I0651363

Mary Bird

The Hawkshawes

A Novel. Vol. 1

Mary Bird

The Hawkshawes
A Novel. Vol. 1

ISBN/EAN: 9783337273484

Printed in Europe, USA, Canada, Australia, Japan

Cover: Foto ©Andreas Hilbeck / pixelio.de

More available books at **www.hansebooks.com**

THE HAWKSHAWES

A Novel

BY

M. A. BIRD

AUTHOR OF "SPELL-BOUND," "THE FATE OF THORSGHYLL"
ETC. ETC. ETC

IN TWO VOLUMES

VOL. I

LONDON
JOHN MAXWELL AND COMPANY
122, FLEET STREET

M DCCC LXV

CONTENTS

OF

THE FIRST VOLUME.

CHAP.   PAGE

   I. FUNERAL AND DEATH 5

  II. THE CONSEQUENCES OF ADVERSITY . . . 21

 III. THE FALSE FRIEND, AND THE TRUE ONE . 42

 IV. ELLEN BEGINS THE BATTLE OF LIFE. . . 63

  V. ELLEN IS INTRODUCED TO THE HAWKSHAWE

      FAMILY 86

 VI. AN ASTONISHING PUPIL 111

VII. AN UNNATURAL COMBAT 131

VIII. A MYSTERIOUS VISITOR, AND A TALE OF

      HORROR 154

 IX. THE DEATH WAIL. 194

  X. WHY THE DEATH WAIL WAS HEARD . . 212

iv CONTENTS.

CHAP.   PAGE

XI. THE GRAVE BY THE SEA 235

XII. LOVE AND LEARNING. 254

XIII. HOW ELLEN'S LETTERS WENT ASTRAY . . 275

XIV. REGINALD LOSES FAITH IN HIS TUTOR.—A
      VISIT TO THE HERMITAGE 293

THE HAWKSHAWES

CHAPTER I.

FUNERAL AND DEATH.

THERE was not a dry eye among the whole congregation when the funeral sermon was ended.

Every one knew the sterling worth and goodness of their late pastor; and, as his old friend, who preached the funeral sermon, and who had travelled many hundred miles to perform this last sad office, gave his simple testimony to his virtuous life, beginning from their school days, and embracing a period of nearly fifty years, all knew that the speaker stated but the simple truth, and was not led into extravagant eulogy by the warmth of his friendship.

The sorrowful assembly quitted the church. The preacher, after a short rest and much-needed refreshment at the parsonage, was compelled to hasten back to his own parish; and the widow and her only child were left alone.

It was a lovely, balmy afternoon in September; the gentle west wind, instead of blowing the leaves from the trees, seemed to woo them to remain; the robin sang cheerfully, and the blackbird piped as merrily as though he had the cheerful spring before him, instead of dreary winter.

Mrs. Maynard's naturally fragile constitution was so completely broken down by unceasing attendance on her husband during his last illness, that, though by nearly twenty years his junior, it seemed improbable she would long survive him. The painful excitement of the funeral, and the necessity of exerting herself to pay due respect to the old and tried friend who had been her guest on the occasion, had supplied her with a fictitious strength to undergo the fatigue of the day; but when the rumble of the fly that conveyed the Reverend Mr. Cottingham to the railway station was lost in the distance, she sank quietly back in her chair and fainted. Ellen's loud cry brought the bewildered servants to her assistance, and by their united exertions the poor lady was restored to consciousness.

"I must not give way like this," said Mrs. Maynard, striving to appear stronger than she really felt, "you will not be able to complete your preparations, dearest, if you are called away so often to attend to me. I ought to try to assist you, instead of being a hindrance."

"Do not fret about it, dear mamma," replied her daughter, "you will but make yourself worse by doing so. If we cannot get ready by the time named, it will not be difficult to defer the sale for a few days."

" The sale *must* take place on the day appointed," said Mrs. Maynard, in a weak, but decided voice, " for on the day after, the painters and workmen have orders to commence the repairs."

" So soon!" sighed Ellen ; " then it shall be so. Sit you quietly here, dearest mamma, and I will manage everything."

Two days before that which was fixed for the sale, Ellen had accomplished her laborious duties. Every repository for those odds and ends which careful house-wives delight in accumulating, had been turned out, and its contents examined. Whatever might be useful in the quiet lodgings to which she and her mother had resolved to retire, was retained, and the remainder distributed among the poor.

Mr. Maynard had held the living for more than thirty years, and as his wife was one of those careful women who, under the idea that it "may be useful some day," never throw anything away; and as her feeble health had prevented the wholesome clearance effected by an occasional active rummaging, the accumulation of useless rubbish during this long period was something enormous. There were bundles upon bundles of old letters, possessing the peculiar charm of being of no use or interest *even* to the owner; account books that ought to have lighted fires twenty years before; piles of Ellen's own copy books, just as they had been sent from school; and bales and boxes of garments of so ancient a cut that one might have been puzzled to decide whether they might or might not have been acceptable at the British Museum.

All was at length completed. The auctioneer's clerks had marked and catalogued the furniture, excepting a few favourite

articles, such as her father's easy-chair,
which had been removed to their lodgings,
and Ellen had now only to support her
mother's feeble steps from the home which
had been hers for so many tranquil and
happy years.

Mrs. Maynard was sitting at the open
window of her favourite parlour, looking
into the garden. The window was deeply
set in a thick mass of roses, clematis, and
sweet briar, and the well-known perfumes
stole into the room, filling it with odours
as sweet as when their first blossoms opened
with not more joyous aspirations than those
of the faded and withered woman who now
inhaled their fragrance for the last time.

" I must walk round the garden once
more before I go, Ellen," said Mrs. Maynard, rising from her chair with more activity than she had shown since the day of
her husband's funeral.

"Nay, dear mamma, do not attempt it now," remonstrated her daughter; "wait till you are stronger."

"No, darling," said her mother, firmly, "when once I go away, I shall never set foot in my old home again. I could not bear to see alterations made by strangers in the spots that your father loved. I could not bear to see the shrubs that he planted cut down to make way for modern improve- ments. I shall always think of the dear old garden as it was when he cultivated it,— full of sweet, homely English flowers, and the trees and shrubs, whose growth we watched together for so many years. I will walk round it, if possible, this evening; and that will be for the last time. I shall never come into it when it belongs to strangers."

With great difficulty the sorrowing widow went through her self-imposed task. Ellen

had thoughtfully brought with her a camp
stool, that her mother might rest herself
occasionally.

"Do not gather any flowers now, dear
mamma," said Ellen, as her mother
stooped painfully, to pluck a rose of remarkable beauty; "I will run out again
while you rest after this fatiguing·walk, and
gather all your favourites. I'll not miss
any, I assure you."

"I can trust you, dear," replied her
mother; "but here is one that I must
gather with my own hand; the latest bud
on your poor father's favourite rose-tree.
When it withers, preserve it in memory of
this day, my dearest Ellen; it is the last
flower I shall ever give you out of the old
garden."

Ellen did not trust herself to reply, but
strove hard to keep back her tears, while her
mother fixed the half-blown rose on her
bosom.

"I must go in now," said the poor lady, "for I feel quite exhausted."

With the tenderest care Ellen supported the feeble steps of her beloved parent back to the parlour; the only room in the house in which the furniture remained undisturbed. She placed her comfortably on the large old-fashioned sofa, and having received an assurance that she felt better, and was only suffering from fatigue, ran out into the garden to cull the bouquet. In about twenty minutes she returned, laden with her fragrant burthen, and just as she re-entered the house a servant met her to say that the fly which was to convey them away was waiting at the door. With a sad heart, struck down by this last trivial incident, though it had occurred in consequence of her own orders given in the morning, Ellen went into the parlour.

Another had entered before her.

The fly had come with its rattling wheels,

and Betsy had hastened to announce its
arrival. But an angel with noiseless wings
had come into the house. It had gone forth
again unnoticed. The rustle of its pinions
—dark when viewed from this lower earth,
bright and glorious when seen from above,
with the light of heaven streaming upon
them—had not been heard by the ears
that were so ready to perceive the
rattle of carriage wheels on the pave-
ment.

It had gone forth again, with another,
a suffering spirit, in its arms; and no one
saw it.

"Hush!" said Ellen, as she looked into
the parlour; "hush, Betsy! Mamma is
asleep. Tell the man to wait. I would not
disturb her on any account."

Poor loving child! Thou couldst not, if
thou wouldst!

Ellen arranged her flowers, and waited
patiently. Minute after minute glided by.

Her mother was not accustomed to sleep so long in the daytime; but doubtless she was much wearied.

"It is very strange," murmured Ellen; " I hope she has not fainted."

She held her face close to the parted lips, but she felt no breath ; she gently touched the pale cheek—it was cold as marble; she tried to raise the hand, but it was rigid. Only once before had she looked on Death, and now she hesitated to recognise his grim and unfamiliar presence. She flew to the front door.

"Fetch a doctor!" she cried to the driver of the fly, who was improving the occasion by polishing the brass on his harness— "Mr. Smedley, if he is at home; and if not, then the first you can find. Make haste ! Drive as fast as you can, and bring him back with you. My mother is very ill!"

She hastened back to the parlour, and saw Betsy standing by the sofa.

" Is she recovering?" was her first eager
question. " Run to the door, Betsy, and
hurry the man off! How slow he is!"

Betsy obeyed in silence.

"Make haste for the doctor, Jim," said
she to the driver (an old acquaintance);
"it's of no earthly use his coming, but it
will satisfy miss. Poor dear missis is
gone, but it will be best for the doctor to
tell Miss Ellen so himself; so don't lose no
time."

" Betsy—look here!" said the young lady,
turning round a face of ghastly paleness as
the faithful servant returned to her; " do
you think it possible that—but I cannot
believe it! I am sure she has only fainted."

" The doctor will be here soon, miss,"
replied the girl, " and he will know better
than I can what is amiss. She's very pale,
and she's very cold; but while there's life
there's hope, you know, miss."

" But what if there should *not* be life?

What then, Betsy?" said poor Ellen, in a sepulchral whisper.

Betsy either did not or would not hear the question, but busied herself with the well-meaning mockery of administering restoratives, until the arrival of Mr. Smedley, the surgeon who had attended Mr. Maynard during his last illness.

"What is amiss with mamma?" cried Ellen, as the surgeon bent over the sofa; "is it a fainting fit?"

"No," he replied, shaking his head; "no, it is not a fainting fit. Prepare yourself for the worst, my dear young lady; I can give you no hopes of her recovery. You have long been aware that she had disease of the heart, which might prove fatal under any strong excitement. I did not expect her to survive your father, even for an hour. That she did so was little short of a miracle; and now this last grief of leaving her home has been too much for her. It would be

worse than useless for me to offer any consolation at present, but you may rely upon
my putting off the sale, and doing everything that is requisite to spare you every
avoidable pain and trouble."

He paused on perceiving that his words
fell upon unheeding ears.

" Tell her," he continued, to Betsy—" tell
her, when she is sufficiently composed to
understand you, that she may rest perfectly
satisfied that everything shall be attended
to.   I am now going to the auctioneer to
stop the sale.   I will return in an hour,
and ascertain her wishes respecting the
funeral."

It seemed that the presence even of the
kind-hearted and sympathizing doctor was a
bar to the full indulgence of the orphan's
grief; for no sooner was the door closed
behind him, than Ellen uttered a wild
scream, and threw herself sobbing upon the
body of her mother.

The violence of her sorrow at length exhausted itself, and her own strength with it; and when Mr. Smedley again presented himself, she wore an outward appearance of calmness which he had little expected to see. When he talked to her, however, of the arrangements which he had already made, and consulted her as to those which he contemplated, he found her quite incapable of comprehending what he said, or of forming any opinion upon the subject.

" Have you any relations to whom I can write?" he asked. " You ought to have some friend at hand to act for you."

This question was heard and understood.

" Friend! Relation!" she repeated, looking round with a frightened air, " I have not one, now *she* is gone! Oh! it is dreadful to be all alone in the world!"

Mr. Smedley was glad to see that another idea, even though a painful one, had dawned

upon her mind. She wept afresh at the
sense of loneliness, and his kind condolence
soon aroused a feeling of gratitude, that all
unconsciously to herself soothed the in-
tensity of her grief.

CHAPTER II.

THE CONSEQUENCES OF ADVERSITY.

In little more than a week after her father's funeral, Ellen Maynard saw the remains of her beloved mother deposited in the same grave; and on the evening of that day she went alone to the lodgings which had been prepared for the reception of her mother and herself.

The sale took place in due course, and then, on examining the state of her exchequer, Ellen found that instead of the comfortable independence which all the town had expected would have been hers, either at her father's death, or when she married, something under a thousand pounds

constituted her whole fortune, for Mrs.
Maynard's private income expired with
her.

Ellen was too unsophisticated, too free
from all worldly-mindedness to think it
prudent to conceal from her acquaintances
the fact of her altered fortune. She suffered
it to be fished out of her by one of the first
visitors who called upon her in her new
abode, and in a few hours it was known all
over the town. She was made unpleasantly
aware of the error she had committed, by
the patronizing airs which some subsequent
visitors assumed towards her, and by the
humiliating freedom of the advice which
almost all thought themselves entitled to
obtrude upon her ; one indeed going so far
as to hint at the usefulness of left-off wear-
ing apparel. Now Ellen, though a gentle
and affectionate girl, was a very proud one,
and these things galled and chafed her more
than she liked to own, for such a spirit was

not, she knew, in accordance with the precepts of Christian humility which her
parents had always endeavoured to incul-
cate in her mind.

"And now, my dear Miss Maynard,"
concluded the last-named visitor, after a
great deal of unasked-for advice upon the
subjects of propriety and economy, "if
there is anything that I can do for you, only
let me know it, and if it lies in my power to
befriend you, you may reckon upon me;
and I may as well just mention that we are
going out of mourning next week, and if
there is anything that would be useful, you
know, and the things are many of them as
good as new, and my girls are nearly of
your own height——"

"I feel much obliged to you, ma'am,"
interrupted Ellen, swallowing a lump in her
throat that seemed threatening to suffocate
her, while her eyes flashed, and her lip
curled, though she felt ready to burst into

tears, "but I have already provided the servants with more mourning than they will require, as they are not going to continue in my service."

"Oh, indeed!" said Mrs. Minshull, very curtly, for she felt rebuffed, and though she could hardly suppose that the poor orphan had wilfully ignored the drift of her beneficent offer, there was something in Ellen's manner that prevented her explaining herself more clearly; "then, if there is nothing I can do for you at present, my dear Miss Maynard, I will wish you good morning. Remember you may always look upon me as a friend. You are very young to be thrown, as I may say, almost penniless upon the world; and whenever you need it, my best advice is at your service. By-the-bye, my dear, I may as well ask you now what are your plans for the future?"

"Really, madam," replied Ellen, almost out of patience, "I have not had time to consider for the future. My thoughts have been so painfully engrossed by the past, that nothing short of absolute necessity could have compelled me to pay attention even to the present. Of the future I have scarcely thought."

"Well, my dear girl," said the visitor, rising, " all I can say is, do nothing without consulting your friends. Good morning, my dear—good morning."

She departed, and Ellen sank back in the comfortable easy-chair—now, alas! her own —and large tears rolled down her cheeks.

" *Friends!* consult my *friends!*" she murmured—"where are they? Misfortune has shown me that I have none—except, indeed, Mr. Smedley; he is a friend. And, besides——I wish I could hear whether Lady Willoughby has been seen in the town for the last day or two. I did not like to ask any of those gossiping, patronizing women. Oh! I must not say I am friendless!

While dear Frank lives I have one friend
worth all those I have forfeited by the crime
of poverty. And his mother is my friend,
too, I am sure she is," she added, with a
dubious sigh.

Ellen fell into a reverie, from which she
was roused by the entrance of Mr. Smedley.
The face of the good doctor expressed concern, and some vexation. He tossed his hat
upon the table, and flung his gloves into it,
as though he wished somebody's head were
in the hat, and the fists of a pugilist in the
gloves. Having done this, he took a chair
in silence.

" What is amiss, my dear sir ?" said
Ellen. " You are certainly vexed about
something."

" Yes, my poor child; I am vexed with
you, but downright angry with myself."

He had never before addressed her so
familiarly; and the first suggestion of her
sensitive pride was — " And is _he_, too,

changed with changing fortune?" But also he had never before spoken to her so kindly; and pride, as it deserved in this instance to be, was put to the rout.

"What have I done wrong?" she asked, mildly.

" You have let some confounded gossip get hold of the fact that you are not so rich as you were supposed to be; and it is buzzed all over the town by this time."

"I know it," said Ellen, quietly; "and at first I regretted it, because I was exposed to much petty annoyance in consequence; but now I am glad it is known. It has shown me the true worth of many professing friends. I am saved the disgrace which I should incur in my own eyes were I, even tacitly, to countenance a falsity; and besides," she added, with a smile of lurking sarcasm, " it has procured for me the benefit of more good advice than I shall be able to follow if I live to the age of a hundred."

"I'll be sworn it has!" cried Mr. Smedley, laughing; "and that, my dear young lady, tallies curiously with the petty annoyances that you mentioned in the first instance. Is there any connexion between the two, eh?"

"I cannot deny it," she replied; "but does it not seem strange that the fact of my being poor instead of rich, should give every person an imaginary right to direct and control my actions? And the diversity of their counsel, too, was most amusing; or would have been so, if anything could amuse me now. One advised me to invest my money in a benevolent society, and live upon the proceeds in a highly respectable ladies' school to which she would recommend me. Another almost ordered me to place my little property in her husband's hands, promising a handsome interest upon it, whereupon I was to board in a farm-house in South Wales. A third told me the only thing was to emigrate to New Zealand,

and promised me letters of introduction to
the principal clergy, including the bishop.
A fourth recommended Australia, but
warned me against America. A fifth
asserted as stoutly that America was the
only place ; and a sixth was for starting off
forthwith to order my outfit, and secure my
passage to India. There were but two
points on which they all agreed."

"And those two were?——" suggested
the doctor.

" One, that the utmost circumspection
and propriety of conduct was indispensable,"
said Ellen; " and the other that I must do
nothing without consulting my friends, at
the head of whom I was, of course, to rank
the lady who happened at that moment to
be favouring me with her advice."

" And I," said Mr. Smedley, " whose profession it is to give advice, am now enraged
with myself, because I neglected, or I should
say more correctly, abstained from obtruding

it upon you, on this very subject. I was about to warn you not to let your altered circumstances be known, but I checked myself, thinking I had no business to interfere; but when I heard the way in which these fine ladies talked about it, I was mad to reflect that I might have stopped it all by a few words in season."

" It is better as it is, sir," said Ellen; " the few who are true will seem all the brighter by the contrast, and fortunately my feelings are not at all involved so far. There is not one among them all for whom I felt any affection."

She paused a moment, and then asked, with some hesitation, if he knew whether Lady Willoughby had been lately into the town.

" Yes—yes—I believe so," replied Mr. Smedley, turning red, and hesitating, " that is—I think not. I was attending her a week ago for a slight attack of influenza."

"Is she confined to the house?" asked
Ellen.

"No—no—not now," stammered Mr.
Smedley.

There was something very suspicious in
all this hesitation on the part of a man
usually so frank and free-spoken as the
doctor; but aided by her experience of
other "dear friends," the orphan saw plainly
enough what he kindly desired to conceal.
Lady Willoughby was able to visit her, but
held aloof. This was worse than if she
had come, like the rest, with her budget of
advice, for Ellen could have taken advice
from *her*, as from a mother. This was
indeed the unkindest cut of all. Ellen, it
is true, had formed no plans for the future;
but she had indulged a hope and a dream.
The hope was that Frank Willoughby—a
captain in the army, and now at Malta with
his regiment—would keep true to the faith
he had plighted to her in more prosperous

days; the dream was, that his mother, who had not found anything to object to in a marriage with the daughter of a clergyman, who, however moderate and simple his own style of living, was known to have saved up something handsome for her wedding portion, would not now look upon it as a *mésalliance* not to be thought of for a moment.

Lady Willoughby and Frank were the two ingots of refined gold which she had fondly thought would remain to her, after the fire of adversity had melted the dross away.

The doctor's hesitation dispelled the dream; but she clung with renewed tenacity to the hope.

Mr. Smedley had heard rumours of the engagement between Captain Willoughby and Miss Maynard; but he knew too much of the world, and of Lady Willoughby's worldly nature, to feel any doubt as to the

course she would pursue under the altered
circumstances. And so, between his wish
to prepare Ellen for what was to come, and
his fear of inflicting pain upon her, he
hesitated and blundered, and looked uncomfortable; and without assuming to be
in the secret, and so having the privilege of
condoling with her, he conveyed the hint,
and expressed his sympathy, as effectually
and delicately as the most skilful diplomatist
could have done. Perceiving that Ellen
remained silent and thoughtful, he withdrew on the plea of professional business,
and stepping into his gig, drove off to
Willoughby Court.

Her ladyship was at home, and received
him most graciously.

" Oh! my dear doctor!" she exclaimed,
with a great deal of affable condescension,
" you are the very man I most wished to
see!"

" I trust your ladyship has not taken a

fresh cold," said Mr. Smedley. "What sort of night did you pass?"

"Wretched! wretched!" sighed her lady-ship, in tones of the deepest self-commisera-tion.

"Cough troublesome?" suggested the doctor.

"Not very. It was the mind—the mind, doctor," said she, shaking her head tragi-cally.

"And in what way can I 'minister to a mind diseased?'" he asked.

"I think you can, my good sir," she said; "it is all about that poor unfortu-nate girl, Miss Maynard. You see her frequently, I believe?"

"I have just left her," he replied.

"Were you aware of the existence of a silly sort of romantic, childish affection, or rather I should call it flirtation, between her and Captain Willoughby, before he went abroad?" asked her ladyship.

"I have heard of it, certainly," said Mr. Smedley, coldly, "but as a serious engagement, sanctioned by both families; and not by any means as a romantic, childish affair."

"Well, I must confess I was so foolish as to let it pass at the time," said her ladyship. "I looked upon it as a mere boyish fancy on Frank's part, that he would get over as soon as he saw a little more of the world."

"And did not your ladyship take into consideration the effect all this might have upon Miss Maynard?"

"Oh! my dear sir," simpered Lady Willoughby, with an affected little laugh, "young ladies don't die for love now-a-days!"

"I would not undertake to say that," said the doctor, gravely; "though I think Miss Maynard has too much pride and dignity of character to die, even if she were jilted."

"Jilted, sir!" repeated the lady, indig-

nantly, "do you mean to apply that term to
my son?"

"No, madam; for I have too high an
opinion of him to think he will do anything
to deserve it," said the provoking doctor.

The lady fidgeted, and looked uneasy.
Then taking up a letter from the table
beside her, she continued, "Whatever your
opinion on that point may be, doctor, I rely
upon your preserving the strictest secrecy
concerning what I am about to communicate to you. I especially wish that
Miss Maynard may not become acquainted
with it."

"Madam," he replied, "a secret with me
is always inviolable."

"I know that, my dear sir, I know it
well," said the lady in her blandest manner,
"and therefore it is that I wish to confide
in you; besides which, you are such a friend
to poor Miss Maynard! This letter is from
my son. It arrived yesterday evening, and

in addition to the awkwardness of my relations with the poor dear girl, was the cause of my rest being so broken last night."

"I trust Captain Willoughby is well?" said Mr. Smedley, hastily, for he liked and esteemed the young man as much as he contemned the paltry pride of his mother.

"Yes, thank Heaven! He is quite well," replied Lady Willoughby; "but he talks so extravagantly about his ' sweet Ellen,' as he calls her!—and he has even enclosed a note, with a hundred apologies for its brevity, as the mail was just closing. Of course I cannot think of giving it to her, under the present altered state of affairs; but what am I to do?"

"I should imagine the course was quite clear," said Mr. Smedley; "as your son is of age, and entitled to judge for himself, you have nothing to do, it seems to me, but to deliver the note to the young lady."

"But he does not know what a change

has taken place in her circumstances," said her ladyship; "formerly, though the match was by no means so good a one as he had a right to expect, it was not so outrageously bad. She came of a good family, and we expected would have had at least ten thousand pounds; but her foolish father chose to lend it to that speculating cousin of his, and it is all lost, so that I understand she has only a few hundreds left. It is really most embarrassing."

"I never heard Captain Willoughby accused of being a fortune hunter," said the doctor, knitting his brows; "and I neither can nor will believe it of him, even if his own mother says so. I presume that he loved Ellen Maynard's self, and not Ellen Maynard's money-bags; and I am sure I only do him justice, and give utterance to his own sentiments, when I say that if he had heard of the calamities that have fallen upon her, his expressions of affection would

have been much more tender than they are;
nay, that probably he would have written
the long letter to her, and the note and
apologies to his mother."

"Sir!" exclaimed Lady Willoughby, angrily, "you presume upon my condescension in asking your advice and assistance."

"No more, madam, than when I give
you a nauseous draught when you ask my
advice on other matters," retorted the
doctor; "I counsel you, in either case,
according to my best judgment of what is
right and fitting."

"You are a very obstinate man!" said
the lady, forcing a smile, and assuming a
playful tone; "but in the present instance I
really do not want your advice so much as
your assistance. Will you give me that?"

"I'll give no pledge in the dark," replied
the cautious adviser; "tell me what you
want, and I'll tell you just as promptly
whether I can do it or not."

"I want you, then, to intimate to Miss Maynard, as a friend to both parties, that this foolish engagement must be broken off."

"I am sorry that I cannot comply with your ladyship's wishes," said the doctor; "in the first place, as Miss Maynard has not taken me into her confidence, nor even in the remotest way alluded to her engagement, it would be very indelicate in me to begin advising her upon the subject."

"But, my dear sir, as coming from *me*," interrupted Lady Willoughby.

"But, my dear madam," interrupted Mr. Smedley in his turn, "my acquaintance with the young lady does not warrant any such interference; and, in the second place, I could not undertake this very disagreeable office as a friend to *both* parties, unless authorized by at least one of them. Now, my firm conviction is, that I should be doing precisely the reverse of what Captain Willoughby would desire."

"But *I*, sir," she exclaimed, snappishly, "*I* authorize you."

"Am I to understand that it was your ladyship to whom Miss Maynard was to be married?" asked the doctor, drily.

"Sir," cried the lady, starting up in a violent passion, and ringing the bell in a way that accorded with her temper, "I see that your intention is to annoy and insult me. I wish you a very good morning!"

And, as if to show that the conference was at an end, and at the same time to signify her utter contempt for her visitor, she took up a book, leaned back in the corner of the sofa, and pretended to be wholly unconscious of his presence.

The doctor, in nowise disconcerted, and with a curl of the lip that would have made her mad if she had seen it, so expressive was it of conscious superiority, made her a sarcastically profound bow, and departed.

CHAPTER III.

THE FALSE FRIEND, AND THE TRUE ONE.

As soon as the door closed behind Mr. Smedley, Lady Willoughby flung upon the table the volume she had pretended to be reading.

"There is nothing left for it now," she soliloquized, "but to see the girl myself, and try to bring her to reason. It is very provoking! I had counted so fully upon Smedley's help, and there is no one else whom I should dare to trust. Sewell, as a lawyer, would be the most proper person to employ; but then he can't keep a secret from his wife, and she is a walking advertisement. I would not for the world have any one suspect that

I had interfered to stop this match! I should
wish it to be thought her own doing entirely;
and she is far too proud to say anything to
the contrary. Perhaps it will be best, after
all, for me to speak to her, and I'll do it at
once."

As the doctor drove his gig into the town,
Lady Willoughby's carriage swept past him.

"Ay, ay, my lady," he muttered, "go
and do your dirty work yourself. That's
more to the purpose than setting honest
folks to do it for you."

Poor Ellen's heart bounded when she saw
Lady Willoughby's carriage stop at the door
of her abode. She could scarcely refrain
from running downstairs to meet her visitor;
but decorum prevailed, and she sat panting
and blushing, and almost as delighted as
though it were Frank himself who was
ascending the stairs.

As her ladyship entered, Ellen started up
to greet her; but there was a cold, con-

descending, formally sympathetic something in Lady Willoughby's manner that sent the warm blood curdling back to the poor girl's heart.

"My dear Miss Maynard," she began, "I am truly glad to see that you can bear up so wonderfully against your many severe afflictions."

"Miss Maynard!" thought Ellen; then she added aloud, "I have sought for strength and consolation where my beloved parents always taught me to seek them, madam, and where they assured me I should never seek in vain."

"That's right. There is nothing like religion when we are in trouble," said her ladyship, approvingly, as though she were giving her sanction to some remedy for headache, or indigestion; "I should have called on you sooner, my dear, but I have been very ill,—confined to my bed for a whole week,—obliged to call in Smedley."

"Indeed, madam!" said Ellen, with grave
surprise; "I am deeply grieved to hear you
say that." And grieved she certainly was
that Frank's mother should tell such fibs.
She had seen Lady Willoughby, two days
before, coming out of a jeweller's shop; and
as for "calling in Smedley," *that* Ellen
knew to be a favourite pastime of her ladyship.

"Yes, indeed, very ill," said the visitor,
dolefully; "but my own sufferings have not
prevented my thinking a good deal about
you, my dear girl. I have been constantly
wondering what you intend to do, and how
you mean to earn your living."

"Earn my living!" repeated Ellen, va-
cantly, and unable at once to appreciate, in
its full extent, the cold heartlessness of the
woman whom she had learned to regard as
her future mother-in-law.

"Yes, my poor dear, of course it must
come to that," sighed her ladyship, with

affected sympathy; "the trifle, as I understand from Sewell, that has been saved from
the wreck of your father's property would
not be enough to exist upon; but if you
nurse it carefully, it will be something to fall
back upon in a rainy day; and, in the meantime, the excellent education you have received will always enable you to command a
high salary as a governess."

"A governess!" repeated poor Ellen, more
aghast than ever.

"No doubt your proud spirit revolts at the
name, but——"

"No, madam," said Ellen, calmly, and
even with some dignity in her manner,
"pride has nothing to do with it; for my
father always told me that the office of a
teacher—a *conscientious* teacher—was the
most honourable of any; and I remember
that *my* governess was my mother's dearest
friend, and that my father treated her with
the highest consideration as long as she lived.

No—*pride* is not the cause of my emotion.
It is grief—amazement—I scarcely know
what mingled feelings—added to the recollection of a circumstance which *you* appear
to have forgotten,—that I am the betrothed
wife of your son."

"Ah! good heavens!" cried Lady Willoughby, bursting into tears, or affecting to
do so; "surely you cannot be so cruel as to
drag my poor infatuated boy into penury!
If you are capable of such an act of selfishness, you are not the noble-minded girl I
have always taken you for."

"Say no more about selfishness, Lady
Willoughby," said Ellen, in a low but very
firm voice, while her eyes flashed with a
smothered fire; "I see my error now. I
had imagined that I should find you superior
to the rest; but it is not so. Your son, too,
may be but a frothy flake upon the waves
of fortune, that will float from me with the
receding tide; but I cannot believe it—I

think better of him. Amid the general change of all whom I thought friends, I think he, at least, will prove true."

" And you will bind him to his promise, given in a moment of youthful folly," said her ladyship, " and——"

" Pardon me, madam," interrupted Ellen, with a smile of ineffable contempt, " he was four-and-twenty when he gave it, and could hardly plead the indiscretion of youth, were he so mean as to wish it. But I release him from his promise unconditionally."

" Oh! my dear child! Now, indeed, I see you are the same generous Ellen that I have loved so tenderly all her life!"

And the old hypocrite extended her arms to embrace her victim; but Ellen drew back haughtily.

" Hear me to the end, madam," she said; " I will give you no promise not to marry him, if he proves worthy of my affection, and renews his suit to me."

"This is downright impudence!" cried her ladyship, her face swelling with rage.

"No; it is simply justice to Captain Willoughby," said Ellen.

"You must promise solemnly not to write to him," said her ladyship.

"There is no *must* in the case," said Ellen, calmly; "but I shall not write. You may tell him what you like, and give what version you choose of the present interview; if he is what I believe and hope, nothing will alter his opinion of me. In return, I believe his professions of affection were sincere, and I have no right to doubt him, until his own conduct or his own words compel me to do so."

"In plain English," exclaimed her lady-ship, turning pale with anger, "you mean to stick to him like a leech, and set me, and decency, and every kind of propriety at defiance!"

"It is useless to prolong this painful

conference, madam," said Ellen, rising with
great dignity; "if your ladyship were more
composed, I might be able to make you
understand me better; as it is, I shall say
no more than that it is my intention to
leave Stoke Barton to-morrow. I shall not
write to your son, nor communicate with
him in any way, directly or indirectly.
Good morning, madam."

Her ladyship had probably never received
so summary a dismissal since she quitted
the nursery; nor had she ever felt so completely overawed by any one, as she was by
the poor orphan whom she considered unworthy to be the wife of her son.

"Permit me to remark, Miss Maynard,"
she said, gathering herself up, and trying to
assume a manner as dignified as that which
had come naturally to Ellen—"permit
me to remark that if you have the good
fortune to enter the service of a family of
distinction, you must endeavour to observe

a more respectful demeanour towards your superiors, if you desire to keep your place."

By this last broadside of vulgarity she thought she had stricken her adversary to the earth; and sailed majestically towards the door. Ellen quickly opened it, and with a low curtsey, and in a tone, the seemingly unaffected humility of which rendered the sarcasm all the keener, replied, " I thank you for your advice, madam. I trust I shall always treat my superiors with respect, whether I find them in high or humble life."

Lady Willoughby had a great horror of anything which she considered vulgar, so rather than have an altercation on the stairs, she shut her lips tight upon the angry retort that rose to them, and stepped into her carriage.

Ellen watched it from the window, as it whirled away down the street. Two large

scalding tears trembled on her eyelashes.
Pride would allow no more to follow.

"I was prepared to welcome her, and
love her as a mother," she said, "and this
is our meeting, and this is our parting!
And Frank, too—dear, noble-hearted Frank!
How this will grieve him! Perhaps I ought
to have shown more forbearance towards
his mother. But I must not think of that
now; I have too much to do. And there is
Mr. Smedley coming down the street."

Although after her mother's death Ellen
had considerably reduced the quantity of
household goods and chattels which were
reserved from the auction, she still retained
her father's easy chair, and some other
articles too cumbersome to be carried about
with her. These she intrusted to the care
of Mr. Smedley, and received from him the
address of a respectable person in London,
at whose house she might find suitable
lodgings, while seeking for a situation.

The good doctor had seen Lady Willoughby leave the house, and rightly divining the cause of Ellen's flushed face and agitated manner, he forbore to notice it, but listened patiently to her incoherent conversation, and, when she was more collected, gave her some useful hints as to the best means of carrying out her wishes. He particularly recommended her to call upon a religious bookseller, to whom her father had been well known, and through whose influence she would be likely to obtain such a situation as she desired.

There was one thing that Ellen had still to arrange, which pressed heavily on her mind, but she scarcely knew how to manage it. She had resolved not to write to Frank Willoughby; yet she wished to leave a clue to her address, if he chose to seek for it. She could not do this openly without taking Mr. Smedley into her confidence, which would have been anything but agreeable to

her pride and delicacy. Just as he was
bidding her good-bye, despair suggested an
expedient.

"I believe," she said, "that there is
nothing owing either on my dear parents'
or my own account; but as I may have
overlooked some trifle, it will be advisable
to let you know my address wherever I
may go, if you will allow me to trouble
you so far."

"Don't speak of trouble, my dear young
lady," said the good doctor, retaining her
hand while he spoke, "it will be a pleasure to
me to serve you in any way. And I must
confess I was in hopes of hearing of you occasionally, setting aside other considerations."

"Certainly, I will write sometimes, since
you are so kind as to wish it," said Ellen,
with so much smothered emotion that he
saw plainly how friendless she must feel to
be so deeply affected by such a slight mark
of kindly interest in her fate; "and I am

sure I may rely on you not to let my
address or my proceedings be known to any
one in this town."

"I will be careful," he replied, "but
you know it may transpire through other
friends——"

"Other friends!" she interrupted, "oh!
sir, I have none! There is not a single
person in all this place to whom I would
communicate my fate, whatever it might
be, or to whom I would apply for help in
time of trouble."

"Surely you judge them too harshly, my
young friend," said Mr. Smedley. "A whole
townful of people cannot be all bad."

"I do not mean to say they are," replied
Ellen, "but I cannot stay here to seek the
few good ones. Even those whom I found
most unpleasant have doubtless an amiable
side to their characters; in fact I know
they have, for that was the side I always
saw when they were delighted visitors at

4—2

my father's house, and partakers of his
hospitality. Now they are all changed.
Those who used to flatter me seem delighted at the opportunity of overwhelming
me with good advice; nay, in more than
one instance I detected but too plainly a
degree of triumph over my altered fate
that seemed to me almost incredible."

" You will not suspect *me* of taking advantage of any alteration in outward circumstances to give utterance to unwelcome
truths," said the doctor; "and what I am
about to mention may probably throw some
light upon this point. I had so often heard
you accused of being proud and haughty,
that, until I had the pleasure of becoming
acquainted with you, I took it for granted
that such was your actual character. But
when I saw you in your home relations—
obedient to your parents, polite and winning
to your equals, and respectful to your servants—I thought that surely never was

young lady so little understood, or so much
maligned. For a considerable time you
were an enigma to me, until I chanced
to be present on one occasion when
Mrs. Easton called to make inquiries after
your father's health. Now Mrs. Easton
was one of those who had most loudly
found fault with the haughtiness of your
manners, and I was astounded to remark
the servility and obsequiousness of her demeanour towards you."

"Mrs. Easton was a contemptible syco-
phant," said Ellen.

" Precisely so," rejoined the doctor; "but
permit me to say that you were hardly wise
to show so plainly your appreciation of her
character."

"She has fully justified me by her recent
conduct," said Ellen; "from being the most
abject flatterer, no one has seemed to rejoice
so much in my loss of fortune; no one has
assumed so much the airs of a dictatorial

adviser. So far from regretting my rejection
of her flatteries, I assure you that few
things give me more satisfaction, because
she has shown so completely that there was
not an atom of friendliness or real liking
under all her fulsome praises."

"But, my dear young friend," said Mr.
Smedley, "if you had rejected her adula-
tion with less indignant sternness, you
would have found her less willing to crow
over you in your fallen fortunes. I have
known Mrs. Easton do many kind actions."

"Oh, yes!" said Ellen, with a bitter
smile, "her name is always conspicuous
enough on the subscription list of every
charity."

The doctor made a wry face. He felt
he had the worst of the argument.

"I see I must give in," he said; "but
allow me, nevertheless, to draw the inference
to which I was leading, at the risk of your
thinking me, too, an attendant upon fortune's
changes."

"I shall never believe that of you, sir," said Ellen, hastily. "Do you not remember that the first time you saw me, you took me to task pretty sharply for something I had done?"

"I do, indeed, my dear—I beg pardon, I mean my dear Miss Maynard—and I also recollect my astonishment at the meek acquiescence of the young lady of whose haughtiness I had heard so much."

"You told me the truth when others flattered," said Ellen; "and now that the flatterers are all blown away, you have still the right to say whatever you please."

"It is simply this," said Mr. Smedley; "when you are out in the world, and it is of importance to your own interests to win 'golden opinions from all sorts of people,' let flattery pass as part of the current coin of society. If you take it at its true value it does you no harm; and you have seen by experience that a too Roman rejection of it may create enemies."

" I thank you for your warning, sir," said
Ellen, smiling sadly; "but it is needless. I
shall have no flatterers now."

" Don't be too sure of that," said the
doctor. " You may meet with a little of
it, in the form of polite speeches, even from
those with whom you wish to form professional engagements; and then, you know,
if you should start and look indignant——"

" I understand you perfectly," said Ellen,
interrupting him as he hesitated to express
his meaning too plainly, " you mean that
it would be well for me to cultivate more
humility of manner. It is not the first time
to-day that I have been told to behave respectfully to my superiors; but *your* lesson
is given with kindness and delicacy, and I
thank you heartily for it, and will try to
profit by it. And now, my kind friend,
farewell; your time is precious, and I too
have still many things to do. I will keep
you informed of my movements; and you,

I feel sure, will be *very* careful to whom you confide my address."

" I may confide it, then," said the doctor, "if some *very* urgent reason is pressed upon me ?"

" I leave it to your own discretion," said Ellen, hurriedly; " good-bye—good-bye!"

" Good-bye, and God bless and prosper you! You may trust me implicitly," said Mr. Smedley, in a voice choked with emotion.

Ellen listened with a quivering lip till she heard the street door shut behind him, and then throwing herself upon the sofa, she burst into a flood of tears.

" Pride!—yes, still pride !" she exclaimed, starting up, and making a strong effort to overcome her emotion. "The only friend I have! The only one who has not changed with fortune, and I must needs hurry him away lest he should see how keenly I felt at parting with him! I wish he would come back! but I'll be honest upon paper; and when I write I will tell him how grieved I felt when he left me. Yet I wish I could press once more, and more warmly, the hand that ministered to my father in his sufferings, and which alone was extended in true friendliness to his orphan!"

All that night Ellen Maynard spent in packing and preparing for her journey, and at three o'clock in the morning she departed for London by the mail train.

She had never before visited the metropolis; for her father had been too deeply devoted to his clerical duties to leave them while he had health and strength to perform them; and her mother had entertained such a nervous dread of railway travelling, that she was actually kept at home by the very means which should have made her leave it with more ease and frequency.

CHAPTER IV.

ELLEN BEGINS THE BATTLE OF LIFE.

THOSE who visit London for pleasure are
very differently affected by their first entry
into its wilderness of streets, from those who
go there, alone and friendless, to seek a
livelihood.

To the former it is a fairy land of wonder
and delight; to the latter it is a troubled
ocean on which they are putting forth, perhaps without chart or pilot, and with more
or less imperfect sails and rigging.

Hard indeed is the lot of those who are
also without ballast, but such was not Ellen
Maynard's case. She had left the greater
part of her money in the hands of the

lawyer who had always transacted her
father's business, a man for whom she
entertained a high respect in his professional capacity, but for whom she had
so little sympathy or friendship that she
used to describe him as a "respected
aversion."

For her immediate use she had retained
only about twenty pounds, which she fully
expected would suffice for all her wants
until she should be in a position to support
herself by her own exertions.

Ellen was a very steady-minded girl, and
not at all prone to indulge in nervous
fancies; but a sickening sense of loneliness
came over her, as she passed through the
crowds of strange faces, and looking round
at the piles of comfortable houses, knew
that there was not one friendly door to
open at her approach,—not one hand that
would be extended to take hers in a kindly
grasp,—not one eye that would brighten

into recognition when it met hers. Now indeed she felt the full value of Mr. Smedley's kind forethought in giving her the address of a person with whom she could lodge. She found it to be a neat house in a quiet street. The latter quality, however, being merely relative to the more crowded thoroughfares, she did not discover at first, but innocently thought she must have dropped into the very centre of London noise and bustle. Having arranged the terms of her occupancy of a large bedroom, with the privilege of receiving business calls in the parlour, and a moderate scale of charges for boarding with the meek-looking widow who owned the house, she drew up an advertisement, stating her accomplishments, and the profession of her late father, and sallied forth to pay a visit to the religious bookseller, and to beg him to allow the answers to be left for her at his shop.

Mr. Morton received her courteously;

listened to her respectfully; condoled with
her in set terms upon the lamented decease
of her excellent father; gave instructions to
his assistants to take in her letters and give
her address to inquirers; and with many
protestations that he would do everything
in his power to further her interests, bowed
her out. Ellen knew very little of the
world, but she had an intuitive conviction
that before her feet had re-crossed the
threshold, herself, her affairs, and his own
promises, had all vanished from his mind
as completely as last night's dreams. She
had no right to expect anything more on
her own merits—but her father! Alas!
poor Ellen! There her ignorance of the
world became manifest. Her father had
spent his useful life in the unostentatious
performance of his duties. He was not a
popular preacher. He had never had the
honour of delivering an oration before the
Queen, and getting it advertised in the

Times for years afterwards. If he had, a visit from his daughter would have been readily remembered by the religious bookseller.

Ellen returned, sad enough at heart, to her temporary abode. She knew not wherefore she felt more depressed in spirits than when she had set out. Her object was attained, and she was at liberty to use the name of one of the most respectable men in London as a guarantee for her own trustworthiness. She had formed no higher hope before she saw him, and the urbanity of his manners was unexceptionable; but it seemed as though she had come in contact with a moral iceberg.

She spent several days in visiting some of the principal sights and exhibitions. But notwithstanding the lively interest she felt in all she saw, the time passed drearily enough, for she was alone.

Each morning she called to inquire for

letters, and received several from governess
agents, and such folks, but none that promised to lead to the realization of her
wishes.

On the evening of the sixth day she was
setting out to order another insertion of
her advertisement, when a visitor was announced. Her heart beat quick when she
entered the parlour, and found herself in
the presence of a tall spare man of about
forty-five years of age.

His black hair was already grizzled, and
his dark face was deeply lined by the
furrows left by fierce passions or deep
suffering, or perhaps a combination of the
two. His bushy eyebrows overhung eyes
which seemed to pierce into the very
thoughts of the person he addressed, and
which, joined to a high aquiline nose, gave
him as much resemblance to a bird of prey
as it was possible for a very handsome man
to bear.

Ellen did not much like his appearance, and she, moreover, felt somewhat overawed by the steady gaze of those formidable black eyes; but she betrayed nothing of this in her manner, which was quiet and sedate.

"I presume," began the stranger, without a moment's hesitation, "that I have the honour of addressing the lady who advertised in the *Times* for a situation as a teacher?"

"I did advertise, sir," replied Ellen, " and left my address with a bookseller who, having known my father for many years, could answer for the respectability of my family. I can give no other reference, as I have not been similarly employed before."

" But I suppose you have friends in the town where you lived?" said he, inquiringly.

"No—none to whom I would apply in such a case as this," she replied. " I was very differently situated there. I was supposed to be heiress to a considerable fortune, and now, through the misconduct of a relation, I am obliged to work for my own living."

"Have you no other relations?" asked the stranger.

"There is no one with whom I can claim kindred, except the cousin I have just mentioned," said Ellen; "and even if I knew where to find him, I would not apply to him. Not," she added, seeing that an incomprehensible, grim smile curled the visitor's lip, "from an un-Christian spirit of resentment for the wrong he has done me, but because I have every reason to believe that his misconduct was the means of hasten-ing my dear father's death."

"Humph!" said the stranger, "so you have no friends at all? What! Not even a young lady correspondent?"

"I have told you already, sir, that Mr. Morton, from whom you obtained my address, is my reference," said Ellen, with some resentment; "if his testimony is insufficient, it is useless to talk further on the subject."

"Nay—nay—you are too hasty," said the stranger; " and, like most hasty persons, you misinterpret the drift of my observations. You must understand that I have a great objection to change;—it unsettles the minds of pupils, and interferes with their progress. Now, I have generally observed that young ladies leaving home for the first time, as you are doing, are apt to take fright when any difficulty presents itself, and run away home to papa or mamma, or to some dear, kind, misguided aunt or uncle, whose doors are always open to receive them. I was desirous of learning whether you had any such relative, and the discovery that you have not makes me all the more willing to conclude an engagement with you."

5—2

If Ellen had had more experience of the wickedness of the world, this speech would have roused her suspicions; but she only replied, sadly, "I little imagined that my greatest misfortune could be any advantage to me."

"You are a musician," said the gentleman, without noticing her remark; "will you oblige me with a specimen of your talent? The piano does not seem first-rate, but I will make every allowance for that."

Without a word, Ellen sat down to Mrs. Mason's old-fashioned piano, and played from memory one of the most brilliant pieces she knew. Her auditor seemed perfectly absorbed in attention.

"Excellent! excellent!" he murmured; "how came you to think of the drudgery of governess-ship, when you might make your fortune so easily as a concert player?"

"I prefer the quieter life," she said;

" besides, I know my father and mother would have been shocked at the idea of my becoming a public performer. I studied music closely from a natural love of it, and now I shall be fully satisfied if it enables me to earn my bread."

" Earn your bread!" he repeated, derisively; " it should earn you an alderman's feast—no, that's too earthly,—it should earn you nectar and ambrosia, and every delicious fruit of the tropics besides! Will you favour me with something else,— something less brilliant, but more expressive of feeling and emotion?"

She reflected for a few moments, and then played one of those exquisite Songs without Words of Mendelssohn's, in which the inarticulate notes seem labouring to express more than language could utter.

As she played on, the fierce domineering eyes drooped and quailed, and he bowed his head upon his hand, and sighed, and trem-

bled. As she glanced furtively at him, she
wondered why she had felt overawed and
subdued before him. The music formed
round her a magic circle within which
she, the enchantress, stood secure in her
might, and that proud, stern man was but
her vassal and her slave.

" And you sing, too ?" he asked, when the
performance was over.

Without answering a word, she complied
with the insinuated request.

Her voice was full and rich in tone, and
had been carefully cultivated. The song
she chose was a plaintive English ballad,
and she had the good taste not to overload
it with roulades and shakes.

The visitor expressed his gratification
more by manner than words, and after a
while the old fierce look returned to his
face, and his keen eyes again shot through
her.

" It is an actual profanation," he began,

with his grim smile, "to talk of worldly
affairs immediately after listening to such
celestial music; but business *will* be attended
to. Are you willing to enter into an engagement with me to instruct my only son,
a boy whose education has been sadly neglected? and do you consider a hundred a
year a sufficient remuneration?"

Ellen had not thought of aspiring to
more than half that sum, but she took good
care not to betray the satisfaction she felt
at the liberal offer.

" A boy!" she repeated; " I did not con-
template teaching boys. How old is he,
sir?"

" Upon my word, his mother could answer
that question better than I can," replied the
stranger, in a careless tone; " I only know
that he is a sad dunce, though not naturally
a fool; and as he has a passion for music, I
think that may be made very serviceable in
bringing forward his mental powers, and

inducing him to attend to his studies. Now, as I am compelled to come to a conclusion this evening with you or another lady, I must trouble you for a prompt reply."

" Then, sir, I must say I see no reason for declining the engagement," replied Ellen.

" Very good," said the stranger; " now we had better make a memorandum in writing, and then there can be no mistakes or misunderstandings afterwards. May I trouble you for pen, ink, and paper?"

Ellen placed writing-materials before him.

" We had better make the agreement for a twelvemonth," said he, after he had written the words, *I, Reginald Hawkshawe,* " or I will pay you a year's salary in advance, if you prefer it."

" That is quite unnecessary, sir, thank you," said Ellen, who saw nothing but kindness and liberality in this proposal; " I am in no want of ready money."

"Very good," said Mr. Hawkshawe, and proceeded to pen a very concise agreement, by which he bound himself under a penalty of five hundred pounds to retain Ellen in her office for a whole year; and then he wrote out a similar document which bound her to remain as teacher to his son for the same period, and under the same penalty.

"There," he said, after he had read them rapidly over to her, "now you may feel that you have something to rely upon. I cannot play any shabby tricks, even if I wished it. Just put your name to this little document, and it is done."

Most people have a nervous dread of *signing their names* (it would be well for some if the instinctive repugnance were a little stronger!), and Ellen did not see the use of this solemn, written agreement.

"I really do not think this is at all necessary," she said, as she turned the paper over and over.

"It is entirely for your own benefit," said Mr. Hawkshawe, in the tone of one who felt hurt by an unjust suspicion; "I should advise you to sign it. But do just as you please."

He turned to look out of the window, and in a moment his quick ear detected the scratching of the pen as Ellen wrote her name.

"That will do," said he, folding the papers; "you will keep that, and I this. And now, as I have imperative business that calls me home this evening, I shall be glad if you can accompany me. Have you any friends whom you wish to take leave of?"

"I have no friends in town," replied Ellen; "but I should like to call and thank the bookseller for obtaining me a situation so promptly."

"I was informed at the shop that he is gone to Paris for a few days," said Mr.

Hawkshawe, "so it's of no use to call. Write to him; that will do as well. Your luggage is, no doubt, all ready for packing. Can you complete your arrangements," he said, looking at his watch, "and be off in half an hour?"

"That is a very short notice," said Ellen, dubiously. "I must settle with my landlady before I go, and she is from home, and may not be back in time."

"Will five pounds cover the debt?" he inquired.

"It cannot amount to half so much," said Ellen. "I have been here but a few days."

"Then, as time is just now more precious to me than anything else, permit me to pay the penalty of my haste," said he, taking a five-pound note from his pocket-book; "enclose this for her to cover all expenses, and compensate for your abrupt departure."

"Thank you, sir," said Ellen, rather

haughtily, "but I prefer paying my own bills."

"Nay—it is but just that I should pay this," said Mr. Hawkshawe, "for it is to accommodate myself."

"I will at least defer it to the last moment," said Ellen, "and in the meanwhile I will get my luggage ready."

She made a slight inclination, and left him to his own reflections. These seemed agreeable enough, for he smiled and even laughed softly as he paced up and down the little parlour.

As time flew on he looked at his watch, and when it wanted only ten minutes to the completion of the half-hour he went out, and speedily returned in a cab.

"Will one cab be sufficient to convey all Miss Maynard's luggage?" he demanded of the servant.

"Oh, la, yes, sir," replied the girl. "She only brought two big boxes and a little one, besides her music."

"Be so good as to tell her the cab is at the door," said he, as he re-entered the parlour and resumed his walk.

Mr. Hawkshawe rubbed his hands when he saw the cabman arranging the young lady's handsome trunks upon the vehicle, and stared when he saw that the " music " was a guitar case, she having said nothing of her proficiency on that instrument.

The half-hour had nearly expired, but Ellen had not yet come downstairs. Mr. Hawkshawe began to manifest strong symptoms of impatience; he looked out into the passage,—placed the bank-note in an envelope ready for her to direct it to the landlady,—listened at the foot of the stairs,—and, lastly, went to the front door, and looked up and down the street, speculating upon every advancing female of respectable appearance, and dreading to see her walk into the house with the air of its mistress.

He was neither a thief, nor (in the

ordinary sense of the word) a swindler, that
he was so anxious to get Ellen off before
the return of poor Mrs. Mason; but he was
fearful lest the good lady, in greater worldly
experience, should prompt her young lodger
to ask him a series of questions which he
desired not to answer, or even to insist
upon a delay, and the production of references, which would have been highly inconvenient and disagreeable.

The last minute of the allotted time was
just expiring, when, to his great satisfaction,
he heard Miss Maynard's voice speaking to
the servant. As he turned towards her, a
lady in widow's weeds, whom he had watched
as she came down the street, entered the
house, and advanced towards Ellen, who
exclaimed, " I am so glad you are come, Mrs.
Mason! This has saved me a world of
anxiety. I have obtained a situation, and
am obliged to set off at once; and I don't
know how much I owe you."

"I'll make out the bill for you in five minutes," said Mrs. Mason, going towards the parlour.

"Five minutes will lose us the train," said Mr. Hawkshawe; "pray say in a word about what the amount is."

"Oh, dear! it puts me in such a flurry! I'm afraid I shall forget something," said Mrs. Mason, nervously. "Let me see— there's ten shillings the room, and six days' board—that's eighteen shillings, you know, Miss Maynard."

"One pound eight," said the stranger. "What else?"

"Oh, yes, I suppose so," said the widow, looking quite startled at his abrupt arithmetic, "but I am so flurried, I really can't reckon. And I think that's all, miss, except washing sheets and towels, and cleaning boots. Because, you know," she added, with a half-sigh, "you only took the room for one week certain."

"Nevertheless, as you would not have turned me out at a moment's notice, I shall pay for another week," said Ellen, placing two sovereigns and a half in Mrs. Mason's hand.

"Thank you, Miss Maynard; but a bargain's a bargain," said the widow, taking the money, however; "I will write you out a receipt directly."

"We shall miss the train!" exclaimed Mr. Hawkshawe, impatiently. "Never mind the receipt."

"Good-bye, Mrs. Mason," said Ellen.

"Good-bye, my dear young lady. I'm sorry to lose you so soon," said the widow, squeezing Ellen's proffered hand; and then drawing her back a little, she added, in a whisper, "Do write a line to me, my dear, just to let me know you are safe and well. I don't half like the looks of him, I can tell you. Did you have good references?"

"References!" repeated Ellen; "no! I did not dream of asking for them."

"Then ask for them now, and wait till to-morrow," said Mrs. Mason; "you can go as well to-morrow as to-day."

"But my luggage!" said Ellen, looking towards the cab.

"Never mind that," urged Mrs. Mason; "have it brought in again."

"It will appear so foolish," said Ellen, with hesitation; "and if all is right——"

"It's all very well to say that," said the widow, nervously; "but suppose all is *wrong*—what then?"

"I must entreat you not to delay any longer, Miss Maynard," said Mr. Hawkshawe, who had missed her, and hurried back again. "Allow me to hand you to the carriage. Good-day, ma'am."

He took Ellen's half-reluctant hand, hurled one look at Mrs. Mason that collapsed her into a state of non-resistance, and bore off his prey.

CHAPTER V.

ELLEN IS INTRODUCED TO THE HAWKSHAWE
FAMILY.

Mrs. Mason, it will easily be perceived, was
not a woman of much energy or decision of
character. Like many persons of her sex
and class, she was apt enough to suspect
danger, but not so prompt in taking mea-
sures to combat it. She looked anxiously
after the cab as it rattled along the street,
muttering to herself, "Dear, dear! if I only
knew what railway station they was going
to! but he told the cabman so low, as if
he was determined I should not hear what
he said."

It was not till an empty cab had passed

in the same direction that Mrs. Mason
reflected that she might have called it,
followed, and spoken to Ellen at the station. But by the time this idea was fully
grasped by her not over-vigorous intellect, the empty vehicle was past hailing,
and that containing the object of her anxiety
had turned out of the street, but whether
to the right or left, she had been too much
occupied with the other cab to remark.

Presently a friend dropped in to tea, to
whom, as a matter of course, the whole
affair was recounted; and as the visitor
possessed a retentive memory, and was
deeply read in police reports, she was at no
loss for dozens of parallel cases in which
young ladies, imprudently advertising for
situations, had been decoyed away, and never
heard of more. There was a curious coin-
cidence in all these adventures, that the
" villain " was never one who might have
pleaded the impetuosity of youth as an

6—2

excuse; but was invariably a man of middle
age; " old enough to know better," as the
gossips very justly remarked.

Whatever might have been the fate to
which they supposed Ellen Maynard to be
consigned, the wildest flight of their imagi-
nations never came near the truth.

She was hurried to the Great Western
Station. The train was just about to start,
and before she had time to ask the name of
the place to which she was going, she had
commenced her journey towards it in a
carriage appropriated to ladies exclusively,
in which Mr. Hawkshawe had placed her,
with every demonstration of its being done
entirely out of consideration for herself,
though she could not help reflecting that
the separation also put it out of her power
to ask him any inconvenient questions.

There was only one passenger besides
herself in the carriage; and as this was
an old lady who was either very cross

or very deaf, Ellen had little prospect of keeping herself awake by a lively or interesting conversation. The old lady snored in a most monotonous and infectious manner, but Ellen resisted the drowsy influence, and kept on the alert to catch the names of the stations at which they stopped, which she did where practicable, by reading the name; and where she could not do this, by trying to decipher the strange sounds uttered by the guards and porters, who seem to imagine that they are calling out the name of the place for the information of the passengers, while for the most part they are simply talking hiero-glyphics.

At one station, however, where they stayed longer than usual, Mr. Hawkshawe appeared for a moment at the door with a glass of hot mulled wine in his hand, which he entreated her to drink. While she sipped it, he ran away to fetch her some sandwiches, and on

his return he had only time to take back
the empty glass and scramble into his own
place before they were off again.

Whatever cause Ellen might subsequently
have for disliking Mr. Hawkshawe, she
never for one moment suspected him of
having put a narcotic into the mulled wine.
If he had guessed that she watched the
stations, and wished her to desist, he could
not have done better than administer that
wicked beverage, which has a soporific
tendency of its own that, under ordinary
circumstances, requires no extraneous aid.

From a deficiency of steam, or some other
cause, the train proceeded more slowly than
usual; the panting of the engine came at
longer intervals; the old lady's snoring was
more prolonged and more somniferous, and
Ellen fell fast asleep.

At the next station a pair of keen black
eyes looked in at the window, and instantly
withdrew, as if fearful of awakening her by

too fixed a gaze. At the next and the next they peered in again exultingly; and at the fourth Ellen found herself, before she could entirely shake off the trammels of a profound slumber, seated in a close carriage by the side of Mr. Hawkshawe.

Though quite bewildered, her first impulse was to look out and see where she was; but nature seemed to be assisting the designs of the strange man in whose power she had so heedlessly placed herself; for, though it was evidently some time after daybreak, such a dense mist hung over the landscape, that it was impossible to distinguish objects a few feet from the carriage.

"Where are we?" was her first very natural question.

"We are in the famous old county of Cornwall," he replied; "we have two or three hours' drive before us, and then we shall be home just in time for breakfast. How pleasant it is to return home after an

absence, is it not?" he added, with a
peculiar mocking laugh.

" Yes," said Ellen, with a deep sigh,
" when there are those to greet us whose
kind voices and familiar faces make the
soul of home. When they are gone, the
mere house is but the dead corpse of home.
I could not bear to go into my father's
house now—

> 'Its echoes and its empty tread
> Would sound like voices of the dead.' "

" I know those lines," said Mr. Hawkshawe; " where do they occur?"

"In Campbell's *Gertrude of Wyoming*,"
replied Ellen; and feeling more disposed
to weep over her own isolated, homeless
condition, than to enter into a discussion on
the merits of the English poets, she leaned
her head against the side of the carriage,
and closed her eyes.

Her thoughts were sad and anxious
enough. There had been a great deal of

haste in taking her from London; and
though Mr. Hawkshawe had stated that
imperative business called him into the
country, there seemed no sufficient reason
why, in these days of safe travelling, she
should not have followed him the next
morning, and had daylight for her journey.
There was also a degree of mystery about
the place of her destination. He had not,
it is true, refused to tell her where she was
going; but he had given evasive answers,
mentioning no well-known locality, but
only the names of obscure villages, from
which she could collect nothing definite,
and also by travelling in a separate carriage had rendered it impossible for her to
follow up her questionings. She was too
innocent and inexperienced to imagine any
intended wrong from all this; but Mrs.
Mason's hastily uttered expressions of fear,
scarcely heeded at the time, had recurred
incessantly to her memory, and roused very

uncomfortable doubts as to her own prudence in concluding such a hasty engagement, and Mr. Hawkshawe's perfect integrity of purpose in urging her to so prompt a departure, and binding her by a written agreement.

However, she was conscious, under her gentle and feminine exterior, of possessing a brave heart, and an unusual endowment of bodily strength and activity; and this, with a firm but not supine faith in a protecting Power above, inspired her with a full confidence that, whatever might happen, she should come off safe at last.

Ellen looked out of the carriage window, and tried to distinguish somewhat of the scenes through which they were passing. There was a vague, hoarse roaring, mingled with the rumbling of the carriage, and now and then she could dimly make out what seemed to be a crag or cliff looming through the fog, which convinced her that they were close to the sea. Presently the mist

began partially to roll away in great cloud-
like masses, giving her short glimpses of
such wild and rugged scenery as made her
heart bound with joy at the idea of being
free to ramble at will, and explore those
romantic heights and gloomy recesses.
Though brought up in a quiet, pastoral
county, she had a great love for wilder and
more rugged landscapes, and the savage
nature of the views she partially obtained
exceeded everything she had ever beheld in
reality or painting. She hoped therefore
that their journey would not be continued
so far as to place this desolate region
beyond a practicable walking distance from
her future abode.

Her wish was speedily gratified, for a
little further on the carriage suddenly
passed under an ancient gateway of ivy-
covered stone, leading into a spacious court-
yard, somewhat roughly paved, and surrounded by buildings. The side facing the

entrance was occupied by a lofty and
very ancient dwelling-house, and all the
rest of the quadrangle was filled with
stables and domestic offices. '

Two stupid-looking lads came out to
take the horses, and a minute later an old
man-servant, with a deeply furrowed face
and white hair, opened a wicket in the
ponderous house door, the two leaves of
which were immediately afterwards thrown
open by a couple of stout country girls.

" Let me welcome you to St. Osyth's
Priory, Miss Maynard," said Mr. Hawkshawe, as he handed her across the threshold.
" Oliver," he continued, addressing the old
domestic, "see that the lady's trunks are
removed carefully to her apartment. It is
ready for her reception, of course?"

" Everything is done as you ordered, sir,"
replied Oliver.

" That is well," said Mr. Hawkshawe.
" Is breakfast ready?"

"It will be served in five minutes, sir," was the reply.

"You will doubtless like to employ the interval in arranging your dress, Miss Maynard," said Mr. Hawkshawe. "If you will have the goodness to follow those young women, they will conduct you to your chamber."

The two stout girls had already, to Ellen's no small amazement, shouldered her two heaviest trunks, chatting to each other meanwhile in a strange jargon which she could hardly comprehend, and were marching away, with the greatest ease, through the large hall, and up a flight of broad stairs.

Ellen followed them. The stairs terminated in a corridor, running round the entrance hall, from which branched off many lofty passages, communicating with the wings and other parts of the house. Into one of these passages the Amazons turned, abating nothing of their speed, nor ceasing

to chatter in their outlandish dialect.
When near the end they went into an
apartment which, as they deposited their
burdens in it, Ellen supposed was intended
for her. It was spacious and lofty, and
the furniture must in former days have
been exceedingly handsome; but all was
faded and old-fashioned, and though it
could not be called exactly dilapidated, the
room had a gloomy and desolate appearance.

"Are you sure you are right?" she asked
of one of the girls. "Is this to be my
bedroom?"

She could not tell whether they understood her or not, for they both together
replied in their strange *patois*, which, for
any intelligence it conveyed to her, might
almost as well have been the vernacular of
the Tonga Islands. Then smiling, and
bobbing several profound curtseys, they
went their way.

Ellen looked round. The clean white counterpane, toilet-cover, and towels, and the fresh water in the ewer, showed that preparations had been made for some one's reception; and although the room was magnificent in its proportions, yet, after all, the furniture was by no means so splendid as to make it unlikely that it might be intended for the use of the governess.

In a few minutes the two girls returned with her guitar case, and smaller luggage, again went through the ceremony of smiling and bobbing, and left her to herself.

After having glanced round the room, Ellen's first impulse was to look out of the windows.

The house on that side was built upon the edge of a precipitous rock, probably for the sake of the natural defence it afforded in the old barbaric times, whence its first construction might be dated. A deep glen, that looked dark and gloomy even at that morning hour, yawned beneath; and amid the crags that strewed its bed, a rapid mountain-stream foamed and roared on its way to the sea, only half seen beneath the many twisted and gnarled old trees that clung to the fissures in the cliffs, seeming to hold on tenaciously by their naked and sinewy roots.

A little below the point at which the house was situated, the glen widened, giving a view of a small rock-bound bay, and beyond, of the wild expanse of the ocean.

Ellen was so entranced by this scene that it was not till the sound of a gong echoed through the vaulted passages, that she recollected that she had to arrange her dress for breakfast. To wash her face and hands, smooth the dark braids of her glossy hair, and generally "settle" her dress, was the work of so short a time, that when one of the girls returned to marshal her to the breakfast-room, she was ready to follow her.

The apartment to which Ellen was introduced corresponded in size, in antiquity,
and in gloominess, with what she had
already seen of the mansion. The table
was covered with a plentiful repast, and a
great deal of massive, antiquated plate; but
what chiefly attracted the young stranger's
attention was the company already seated
at the board.

Mr. Hawkshawe, with a shade more gloom
upon his brow, sat at the head, and on
either side of him was placed a lady. It
needed but one look to see that she who
sat at his right hand must be his mother,
so exactly did her features resemble his.
She was evidently very old, and her once
tall figure was nearly doubled; but her
spirit was as strong, and her mind as active
as ever. There was more vindictiveness
expressed in her face than in her son's;
there was more unbending will about the
compressed lips; there was more fierceness

and penetration in the eyes; in short, she looked like Mr. Hawkshawe converted into a mummy, and possessed by a demon.

The other lady was a woman of a doubtful age; she might be anything between thirty and forty-five; but on another point there was no doubt,—she was insane. A grave-looking, elderly woman stood behind her chair, and directed and controlled all her movements. The poor creature did not utter a word, but quietly obeyed the whispered orders of her keeper. She had one habit, however, which from its wearisome iteration became extremely distressing. She would raise her eyes furtively, by little jerks as though they were climbing steps, till they rested on the countenance of the old lady, when her face would assume an expression of such fear as it seemed impossible she could feel without screaming aloud; but nevertheless she uttered no sound, and the old lady's eyes being always on the alert, quickly detected the scrutiny, and those of the poor lunatic sank under the sharp gaze, only to begin again painfully climbing their imaginary ladder.

As Ellen approached this singular group Mr. Hawkshawe rose and said, " Mother, this is Miss Maynard—Lady Clarissa Hawkshawe. It is needless," he added to Ellen, " to go through any form of presentation to my unfortunate wife, as she is incapable of noticing anything."

" Oh! the new governess!" said the old lady, with a sardonic laugh; " you may be seated."

Ellen had no relish for impertinence, but she could make great allowance for the vagaries of old age; so she curtseyed to the venerable dame, and took the chair that had been placed for her next to the younger lady. She had hoped to see the boy who was to be her pupil, and upon whose dispo-

sition so much of her future comfort depended; but he did not make his appearance,
and she commenced her cheerless meal.

Breakfast passed almost in silence; but
at the very first word which she spoke, in
reply to some question addressed to her by
the master of the house, Mrs. Hawkshawe
turned and looked at her eagerly. Then
her eyes crept back to those of Lady
Clarissa, and fell again into their usual
monotonous exercise.

As Ellen sat there with that evil-eyed
old woman before her, and the poor lunatic
by her side, she recalled, with a feeling of
compassion, the tone of bitterness with
which Mr. Hawkshawe had spoken of the
pleasure of returning home; and she also
thought she saw a sufficient reason for his
wishing to bind her to remain in that dismal
abode long enough to be of some service to
the neglected child, if not to become recon-
ciled by habit to remaining there altogether.

She pictured that child to herself: a pale boy of nine or ten years old, with his mother's mild blue eyes and delicate features; slightly affected perhaps by that fearful malady under which her mind had sunk. And what a home was that for such a child! His mother's insanity, his father's stern melancholy, and above all his grandmother's malignity, composed an atmosphere in which such a young soul must be blighted.

Her fertile imagination soon worked itself into a state of enthusiasm about the delicate little object of her cares, towards whom she inwardly resolved to fill the place of his poor imbecile mother; and when the meal was ended, and Mr. Hawkshawe invited her to accompany him to the study, she rose willingly, notwithstanding Lady Clarissa's malignant chuckling addition of " Ay, ay, Miss Maynard, go to your dear little pupil! He! he! he! You'll find him a sweet docile child, I promise you!"

Ellen curtseyed to the dowager, and as she passed she cast a look of profound compassion on the poor lunatic, who returned it with a gaze of childish wonder, and with a sudden impulse caught her hand, and pressed it to her heart.

"Keep quiet, or I shall lock you up," said the keeper, in a low, stern voice, and the poor creature, trembling with fear, dropped Ellen's hand, and her eyes returned to their old exercise of creeping up to the face of her mother-in-law.

Ellen did not like to mention so delicate a subject to Mr. Hawkshawe at this early stage of her abode in his family, but she felt certain that she could do more towards restoring that poor lady's reason than the authoritative and coercive nurse.

As she followed the master of the house down one of the long passages, he suddenly turned and addressed her.

"You must not take fright at the sight
of your pupil, Miss Maynard," he said, with
an air of embarrassment, though he endeavoured to speak freely; "I warned you
that his education had been terribly neglected."

"Is he—is he—afflicted—mentally?"
she asked, shrinking back, more alarmed
by Mr. Hawkshawe's manner than his
words.

"No, no—he is not insane," replied Mr.
Hawkshawe, "though his temper is very
violent at times. He is merely somewhat
older, and much taller than lads usually
are when placed under female tutelage."

"Then why not have a tutor for him?"
asked Ellen.

"I have tried that, and failed," replied
Mr. Hawkshawe. " He is impatient of
authoritative restraint, but he is easily led,
especially by the power of music—which
is, indeed, the master passion of his soul.

You may bend him to your will by means
of music. It would be difficult," he added,
with an attempt at a laugh, " to find a
doctor of divinity who either could or
would blend melody and mathematics so
dexterously that the pupil would imbibe
the one unconsciously, while eagerly swallowing the other, just as you give a child
a powder in a spoonful of jam."

" Mathematics !" repeated Ellen, still
drawing back,—" I fear you have mis-
understood me, sir. I cannot teach mathematics."

" I do not expect it, my dear young
lady," said he, " I merely named mathematics as the most natural adjunct of an
LL.D. So pluck up your courage, and
come along."

Ellen felt a strange inclination to run
away, and recalled uneasily the sneering
remarks of Lady Clarissa.

" You have not yet told me what you

wish me to teach your son," said she, in order to gain a few moments' delay.

" That is told in two words," replied Mr. Hawkshawe, drawing her arm within his own, and moving onwards;—" you may teach him what you like, and what you can. You will find that you must begin from the very commencement, for he cannot even read or write."

" He must be a mere child, then, after all," thought Ellen; and she went on with recovered confidence.

She soon found herself in a large, airy room, which bore strong evidence, in its furniture and decorations, of having been modernized, so as to render it as cheerful as possible. The windows had been enlarged, and opened to the ground, so that by descending two broad steps, access was gained to a terrace walk, at each end of which a flight of steps led to a secluded lawn and flower-garden, so well sheltered from the sea-breeze by a curtain of cliffs, that all sorts of flowers bloomed there in perfection. The rock was nearly hidden from sight by a belt of tall trees, and the whole scene was so peaceful and lovely as it lay basking in the rays of the sun, now shining forth gloriously, that it looked like a little Eden.

CHAPTER VI.

AN ASTONISHING PUPIL.

ELLEN had barely time, as she passed the windows, to catch a glimpse of the beautiful scenery I have described, for her attention was speedily riveted upon the single occupant of the apartment.

This was a young man who, she was certain, must be much over twenty years old, though every care had been taken to give him an appearance of juvenility. He was closely shaven, but the strong black stubble showed that his beard and whiskers would have grown thick, if allowed. His hair was long and curly, but it was in vain to

attempt, by its careful management, to give
an air of effeminacy to that muscular neck;
and as vain was it to endeavour, by the
boyish holland blouse with its falling collar,
to conceal the herculean proportions of
those broad shoulders, and six foot of
stature.

His face was wonderfully handsome, but—
though his forehead was broad and high—
singularly wanting in intellect. He bore a
strong resemblance to his father, though
with many points of improvement. The
eyes were better set, thus escaping the bird-
of-prey like look which had struck her so
forcibly on the first sight of Mr. Hawkshawe; his nose was less prominently
aquiline, and his lips were fuller and more
curved. He was reclining on a sofa near
the farthest window, and his sole occupation was that of caressing a large dog, on
which his eyes were fixed, with hardly so
much intelligence in them as beamed from

those of the noble animal as he returned his master's gaze.

"Where is your son, sir?" said Ellen, stopping and trembling.

"There," replied Mr. Hawkshawe, pointing towards the young man.

"You have deceived me," she said, in a firm, low tone, though she still trembled; "it is not proper that I should become the teacher of that young man. He is older than I am."

"No, no—you are mistaken," said Mr. Hawkshawe, soothingly; "his appearance is deceptive. I cannot tell his age to a day, but in mind he is a mere child, I assure you."

"You must engage another teacher for him, sir—I cannot undertake the office," said Ellen. "I have been brought here under a delusion. You should have been more explicit with me."

Mr. Hawkshawe's eyes flashed angrily,

and his lips were compressed, and his breath came hard through his distended nostrils; but he controlled his feelings, and said calmly, "You seem to forget the terms of our agreement, Miss Maynard."

"No, sir, I have not forgotten the agreement," replied Ellen; "but I am certain that no magistrate would hold it to be binding."

"How if I should refuse you the opportunity of testing that point?" said Mr. Hawkshawe, through his clenched teeth, while his black brows were ominously knitted together.

"Do you mean to say that I am a prisoner?" asked Ellen, faintly, as she staggered and caught at a chair for support.

"Not if you act honourably, and keep to your engagement," he replied.

"I am not bound in honour to fulfil a promise which was obtained from me by fraud," said Ellen.

"Then you shall be bound by some other means," said Mr. Hawkshawe, looking even more fierce than before. "I tell you, Miss Maynard, I am not a man to be trifled with. Every hope for the future—all that renders the present worth living for—the blighted happiness which forms my sole memory of the past—all hang around that unhappy boy. Womanly tact, aided by the powers of music, *may* rouse him from his mental lethargy, and incite his mind to study. Nothing else has any power over him."

"Then why not employ a woman whose age would be a protection to her?" inquired Ellen.

"Impossible," was the reply, "his hatred of his grandmother is so intense, that an elderly woman would be in danger of her life, if she attempted to thwart or control him.

"I see it all now," said Ellen, as she recalled several incidents connected with her intercourse with Mr. Hawkshawe; "you sought me out partly because I was a musician, but most because I was an orphan and friendless. But you are mistaken, sir," she added, raising her eyes and clasped hands to heaven, "I have still one Friend left to whom I never appealed in vain in time of trouble, and who will not forsake me now, if I remain true to myself."

"Miss Maynard," said Mr. Hawkshawe, solemnly, "have some compassion on the sufferings of a most unhappy father! I tell you again, that boy is the only hope—the only prop of my house. All my other sons have died, just as they gave promise of being all that my heart could wish, and he alone is left to me. *You* can rescue him from the state of mental darkness in which he lives; and will you refuse the sacred office? You ought rather to rejoice at being made the instrument for so divine a work. You ought to look upon it as a holy duty——"

"Pardon me, sir," interrupted Ellen, "you are scarcely qualified to point out the path of duty to others, when you must have greatly failed in your own parental duties before your son could fall into this state."

"Do not judge too hastily," said Mr. Hawkshawe; "it was not my doing. He was stolen when quite an infant, and brought up like a beast, scarcely even learning to speak. Consider well what you have to decide upon. The enlightenment of a human soul in this world, and his welfare in the next, depend upon your exertions. Look at him, as he lies there, caressing his dog. That creature is the only thing he loves, but the existence of that one affection proves that the social feelings are capable of cultivation."

"Why do you not undertake the task yourself?" inquired Ellen.

"He does not love me," replied the father,

sadly; "and besides, I have not the tact and patience requisite for such a task. His teacher *must* be a woman, and a woman with all her fine sensibilities fresh about her;—one who has not been soured by the world; one who has not forgotten the time when she was herself ignorant and foolish; one who will point out his errors without ridiculing them; and lead him to desire improvement, without inflicting on him, by her pedantry, the mortification of conscious ignorance. Such a teacher *must* be a woman, and a young one. Miss Maynard, I have built my hopes on you! Do not annihilate them! There is nothing which you can ask, and I perform, that shall be refused to you, if you succeed in awakening his slumbering mind; and you *will* succeed, if you try in right good earnest."

Ellen's resolution had been wavering for some minutes. Mr. Hawkshawe pressed

his lips upon her hand, and turned hastily
aside. A large tear had fallen upon it.
That tear gained the victory.

"I will try," she said, "but you must
deal fairly with me; and if after a sufficient
trial I fail to rouse his attention, or make
any favourable impression on him, you
must release me."

"I will, but on that condition only," said
Mr. Hawkshawe, who had started round in
delighted amazement at the sudden change,
and was gazing on her with rapture; "and
you must not plead trivial difficulties as a
reason for abandoning your post."

"I think, sir, you would hardly hesitate
to sacrifice my life itself to the accomplish-
ment of your object!" said Ellen, with a
half-scornful smile.

"You are right," he replied, earnestly;
"but I would also sacrifice myself and half
mankind to secure to that boy his natural
and social rights. Nevertheless, you shall

be taken good care of, and your work made as easy as possible. See there, now! he has taken no notice of either of us. He is in one of his sullen moods."

" Is he deaf?" asked Ellen.

" No," replied Mr. Hawkshawe. "All his senses are wonderfully acute. He hears us, but whether he understands our conversation is another question."

Apparently the young man understood enough to comprehend that they were speaking about him, for, with a sullen scowl at his father, he arose and walked towards the door.

" Reginald," said Mr. Hawkshawe, mildly. But the young savage paid no attention to him. " Try the effect of music !" he whispered hastily to Ellen.

She sat down to the grand piano which stood open, and played the first piece that occurred to her recollection. It was one of Chopin's strange mysterious *Nocturnes*, and nothing could have been better chosen. At the first note young Reginald stopped, and turned. With slow steps he advanced towards the piano. He stood by Ellen's side; he watched her hands as with a firm and brilliant touch they danced along the keys. From the hands his eyes wandered up the rounded arms, just visible through the crape sleeves; then up to her face, where the music seemed to be interpreted to another sense, so deeply did she feel every note she played.

Mr. Hawkshawe, as he watched him, might have exclaimed with *Prospero*, " It goes on as my soul prompts!"

When the music ceased, the young man drew a chair to Ellen's side, and said in a deep tone, and with what sounded almost like a foreign accent, " Go on—I want more."

She turned her head with an air of dignity, and looked him in the face. There was no girlish timidity, no shrinking in her gaze. She had once awed an infuriated bull into quiescence by the power of her steadfast eyes, and she now summoned up somewhat of the same expression, and she saw that he was mastered.

"I will play to you again soon," she said; "but now there is something else to be done. There are many things that you must learn; and when you do well I will play to you. But if you displease me I will lock up the piano, and you shall have no more music."

"I *will* have music!" he exclaimed, his eyes flashing, and his clenched fist in unpleasant proximity to her head; "play more *now*—I *will* have it!"

"Would you dare to strike me?" she said, in a low, calm tone; "if you do so, I will go away, and never come back again."

"Don't go away—I will not beat you," said he, "but play to me. I should like to hear your music always."

" That would do you no good," she replied, " you must learn something besides; and I will teach you music when you have learnt other things that will be more useful to you."

" I don't want to learn anything else," he replied, sullenly; " I don't like anything but music;——and Hector," he added, patting the head of his dog, which had jumped on him to attract his notice; " I like Hector."

" Hector is doubtless a noble creature," said the young monitress, " but you would find a much greater pleasure in the companionship of young—young—in the companionship of youths of your own age, provided you knew as much as all boys are taught now-a-days. I can teach you quite enough to make you wish to know more, and then learning will be a pleasure to you."

" I shall never like learning, and I never will learn," said Reginald, doggedly.

" But consider what a disgrace it will be
for a young man of property not to be able
to read and write!" said Ellen.

" I don't care," he exclaimed, with a careless laugh, " the disgrace is my father's, not
mine."

" But the injury falls upon you," said
Ellen.

The words, however, were scarcely uttered,
ere she repented of having spoken them, such
a fearful storm of rage and hatred did they
arouse in the young man's breast. His eyes
flashed, his teeth and hands were clenched,
and his fast-drawn breath whistled through
his dilated nostrils.

" I know it—I know it!" he said at
length, in a deep hollow whisper; " and I'll
have my revenge!"

" It would be wiser to remedy the mischief, for that would be to your own benefit,"
said Ellen, quietly; " and you should remember, too, that you are not the only one who

suffers from your neglected education. How deeply your father is grieved by it!"

"Then why did he drive my mother from his house, to live in the cavern by herself, and bring me up there like a dog?" he demanded, with an air so ferocious that she was almost frightened.

"I know nothing of your family affairs," she replied, calmly; and turning to the piano she played a simple and touching melody. In a moment all his ferocity had left him, and he stood soothed and passive.

"Now," said she, rising, "let us begin our studies; and Hector shall sit beside you. Such good friends should not be separated."

She placed her soft white hand caressingly upon the head of the huge dog, who wagged his tail, and, after looking for a moment intently at her, returned her salutation in a most unexpected and unwelcome fashion, by placing a forepaw upon each of her shoulders, and covering her face by one sweep of his tongue. Young Reginald burst into a loud laugh of delight, as he placed his strong arm behind her to save her from falling; but Mr. Hawkshawe shrieked with alarm.

"Don't touch that brute!" he exclaimed. "Reginald! beat him off! he will kill her!"

But Reginald did not attempt to check his favourite's unruly demonstrations of affection. He merely prevented the young lady from being pushed down, and continued to laugh immoderately.

A change came over the spirit of Hector's emotions.

Mr. Hawkshawe's dread of the animal had yielded in some degree to his fears for Ellen's safety, and he advanced towards her, still calling out to Reginald to beat the dog off. This aroused all Hector's rage, and after showing his white fangs in one terrific snarl over Ellen's shoulder, he rushed past

her, and at the first onset threw Mr. Hawkshawe to the ground. Ellen's movements
were scarcely less rapid than his own. She
clasped her arms fearlessly round the neck
of the fierce animal, but her strength was
not sufficient to do more than embarrass his
attack upon his prostrate foe.

"Help me! help me, Reginald!" she
cried; but Reginald seemed in no hurry to
comply. He rather enjoyed the mortal fear
that was depicted on his father's contorted
features, while he admired the intrepidity
with which that young girl interposed her
own slight form between the enraged brute
and his prey.

At last, seeing that she was nearly exhausted by the violence of her efforts, he
called the dog away, and Ellen rose from
her crouching position so agitated that she
could scarcely stand.

Had she had no one but herself to think
of she would probably have fainted; but

there was a fresh demand upon her energies, and she put off her faintness—as some women can in such emergencies—steadied her nerves by an effort of the will, and instantly recovered her self-possession.

The moment he was relieved from the combined weight of his assailant and his young protectress, Mr. Hawkshawe sprang to his feet, livid with anger, and snatching down a rifle that hung on the wall, hastily examined the priming, and took aim at Hector. Ellen ran towards him.

"If you shoot that dog," she exclaimed, in a low but energetic voice, "you will defeat your own wishes! Your son cares for but two things, and this creature is one of them. The dog has taken a liking to me, and through him I may obtain an influence over his master's mind. If you would not render all my efforts useless, restrain your anger now."

Mr. Hawkshawe lowered the rifle—looked

at his son—then at Ellen, and suffered the latter to take the weapon from his hands.

"I will spare the brute this once, but never again," he said, as he turned on his heel, and quitted the room.

"You are a nice girl. I like you, and so does Hector," said Reginald, coming familiarly up to her, and taking her hand. "Now that the old fellow is gone, come and play to me again."

Ellen was greatly shocked to hear him speak so disrespectfully of his father; but as she knew that his mind was not fitted to receive either reproof or remonstrance, she wisely refrained from uttering either. Knowing also that it would not do for her to exhibit the slightest shade of timidity or fear, she adroitly converted his too familiar clasp of the hand into her own act, and led him with mild authority to the table, where she instantly commenced giving him his first lesson.

It would have been a ludicrous sight to see that stalwart young fellow conning his A B C like a little boy at a dame school; and Ellen avoided this by means of a variety of ingenious contrivances. The most efficacious of these was reading aloud while he followed the words with his eyes, and thus became accustomed to associate the combinations of the printed letters with the spoken sounds.

However, I have no intention of writing a treatise upon education. It is sufficient to say that Ellen, when she had once succeeded in fixing young Reginald's attention, found his perceptions rapid, and his intellect vigorous; and that in rendering her instructions as easy and attractive as possible, she discovered a fund of pleasurable interest in her task, which she had not anticipated.

CHAPTER VII.

AN UNNATURAL COMBAT.

WHILE Ellen and Reginald were still at
their studies, the sound of a gong reverberated through the stone passages, and a few
minutes afterwards the old servant, Oliver,
entered, and announced to Ellen that dinner
would be on the table in half an hour.

"Will you have the kindness to direct me
to my room?" said she. "I came through
so many turninps, that it would take me
half the day to find my way back without
a guide."

"You went first to the breakfast-parlour,
Miss," replied Oliver; "but the direct way
from here to your apartment is quite easy

to find. If you will please to follow me, I will conduct you to it."

Within a few feet of the study-door he turned aside, and led her up a narrow winding staircase, lighted by loop-holes, which showed the enormous thickness of the ancient walls. But modern improvement had been busy here, as well as in the room where she had passed the morning. The rough walls were plastered and painted; the stone steps, worn hollow by the mail-clad heels of many a knight and soldier of the old times of chivalry, had been made level by wooden casings, and thickly car-peted; the loop-holes were glazed, each with a single pane of plate glass; and a silken cord supported by gilded hands, projecting from the wall, served instead of balusters.

"This tower seems very old," said Ellen, with great interest; "I wish that the modern improvements would permit me to see more of it."

" I believe, Miss, it's older than the Conquest," said Oliver, glad of an excuse for resting in the steep ascent; " you can see it in its original state above the first storey, Miss. Master only had it renovated as far as your bed-room. You see the varnish is hardly dry yet, but the smell will soon go off. The workmen had to work hard to get it finished, for they did not begin it till just about an hour or so before master set off to London to fetch you down."

" Indeed! They must have worked very hard," observed Ellen, taking care to betray no astonishment at what she heard, though it revealed to her very clearly that Mr. Hawkshawe had gone to town with the fixed resolution of engaging the " musical orphan" at any price.

" Ah! they knew it *must* be completed before they left off," resumed Oliver, " and the whole twelve who were here, carpenters, plasterers, glaziers, upholsterers and all,

would not have remained here till midnight
—no, not if they'd been offered a hundred
pounds a-piece."

"It is haunted then, I suppose?" inquired
Ellen.

"Oh yes, Miss, so the foolish folk about
here are fond of saying. You see it's the
rats, miss," said Oliver, argumentatively.
"At the foot of these stairs there is the door
leading down to the dungeons of the old
castle—perhaps you remarked it, miss—a
little arched door in the dark recess to the
left as you come up?"

"I saw the recess, but not the door; it
was too dark," replied Ellen, as the old man
paused for a response.

"The door is there, miss," continued
Oliver, "and it's natural to suppose there
must be numbers of rats among the
old dungeons, and then when they get
out and run about the stairs, and make
a noise, people who have not the sense

to know better think the place is haunted."

"I wish *I* could believe so," said Ellen, with a slight shudder, "for I have a great dislike to rats, and no fear of ghosts."

Oliver gave a wistful look at her, and continued his way up the turret stairs.

Ellen found that the first landing communicated by a low arched doorway with the corridor in which her bed-room was situated, thus giving her a short and easy means of transit between her sleeping-apartment and the study. The old man threw open the door, bowed her in with the grace of a courtier of the olden time, closed it after her, and she found herself again in her room with its quaint antique furniture, and rugged prospect.

The idea that she was to sit during dinner under the eyes of that horrible old Lady Clarissa induced Ellen to bestow considerable care upon her dress. This was, of

course, black; but it set off her tall figure,
and pale melancholy face, to the greatest
advantage.

The second summons to dinner had
scarcely ceased to echo through the house
when she descended the stairs.

In the . hall she met Mr. Hawkshawe,
coming, he said, to escort her through the
labyrinth.

Dinner was served in a sumptuous though
old-fashioned style, in a room still larger
than the one where they had breakfasted;
and, from the size of the table, and the
quantity of plate with which it was loaded,
Ellen expected to see several guests. None
however appeared, and she felt herself one
of a very ghastly company, as she sat
down with that hideous old woman, that
stern, unhappy-looking man, and the poor
maniac.

But little conversation passed at table.
The master of the house was gloomy and

taciturn, Lady Clarissa was crabbed and snappish, and Mrs. Hawkshawe only whispered occasionally to her attendant.

Ellen too was silent; not from any sense of awe at being in the presence of her "superiors," for the idea had not once crossed her mind that any one would suppose them to be such;—not from being surrounded by unusual splendour, for she had been accustomed to quite as much elegance, though with less formality, at her father's table; but from the sadness of her own thoughts, and the oppressive dulness that reigned around her.

She could not help contrasting the home of former years—with its comfort, its enlivening converse round the social board, where wit, though abundant, never outraged sense; and conviviality, though under no visible restraint, never trespassed on sobriety; —with the abode where she now found herself, with its frigid state, its grandeur without gracefulness, and its profusion without comfort.

So the day passed on; and many more succeeded it, till the days grew into weeks, and the weeks into months, without any occurrence worth recording.

Lady Clarissa, whenever the governess seated herself at table, directed a searching look upon her costume; and on one occasion, so little did Ellen's dress of rich moire antique suit the old lady's notions of what was fitting and proper, that to it might probably be attributable the more than customary ill-humour which marked her conduct.

Two or three glasses of wine, instead of warming her heart, loosened and sharpened her tongue.

" Did you see those two girls, this morning, with their new fly-away caps stuck all over with artificial flowers?" said Lady Clarissa, addressing her son.

" I saw that they looked very smart," he

replied, "but I did not observe that the improvement was caused by an alteration in their caps."

"*Improvement!*" exclaimed the old lady, angrily, "I wonder what next you'll call an improvement! But I pretty quickly sent their finery to the back of the fire."

"I am sorry to hear that, mother," said Mr. Hawkshawe, "for such an interference was both arbitrary and unnecessary. As long as servants dress in a manner that is suited to their station, it is a wanton infringement of their rights to prevent their indulging in a little harmless decoration."

"It is *not* suited to the station of a servant to dress herself out in silks and flowers," said Lady Clarissa, with a spiteful glance at Ellen; "but there's no knowing where your revolutionary notions may lead to, when you can bring a menial, and seat her at the same table with your mother."

Ellen started, and half rose from her

chair, while the indignant blood rushed to
her face, and her eyes flashed; but reflection came almost as rapidly as resentment,
and she re-seated herself with an air of calm
self-possession that conveyed a better reproof
to the old lady's rudeness than any remonstrance could have done.

Mr. Hawkshawe also started up, but so
much more brusquely that he knocked over
his chair.   Lady Clarissa chuckled malig-
nantly at this exhibition of his wrath, for
it was an agreeable excitement to her to put
him in a rage; he disappointed her, however,
for taking the cue from Ellen, on whom he
cast a glance of profound admiration, he
too resumed his seat in silence, and in the
next moment refilled his mother's glass
with a perfectly steady hand.

" Ugh ! so *you* take lessons, too, I see,"
muttered the spiteful old woman, " and a
very quick scholar you are, that I must
say."

She went on muttering to herself, and
Mr. Hawkshawe had the tact to hasten the
uncomfortable meal to a close, and the good
feeling to draw no more of his mother's
animadversions upon Ellen by paying her
greater attention than was absolutely requisite, confining himself strictly to the barest
civilities of the table, but bowing her out
with marked deference when she retired.

Ellen with difficulty repressed the tears
that were almost choking her, as she hurried
to the study. It was unoccupied; and with
a sudden feeling of release from the painful
restraint that had bound her, she threw herself into a chair and gave way to a passionate fit of weeping.

The low, troubled whining of a dog
aroused her, and Hector laid his head upon
her shoulder, while at the same moment
Reginald pulled her hands from her face,
and looked at her swollen eyes with anxiety
and alarm.

"Who has done this?" he asked, in a hoarse, savage whisper. "Is it my father?"

"No, no," replied Ellen, hurriedly, for the lurking vengeance in his eyes alarmed her; "your father is all that is good and kind."

"Then it is that wicked old hag!" he muttered; "dry your eyes, dear, and don't cry any more. She shall not do it again. I'll go and talk to her about it."

There was nothing alarming in these words, but uttered as they were through his closed teeth, while his face was pale with rage, they recalled what Mr. Hawkshawe had said of Lady Clarissa's life being in danger from the violent hatred which his son bore towards her.

"I did not say it was your grandmother who had made me weep," said Ellen; "and even if it were, you must not harm her. She is very old, and should therefore be treated with respect."

" Yes, she is very old," returned Reginald; " but she is very wicked too, and everybody will be happier when she is dead."

" You must not harm her!" cried Ellen, catching him by the arm as he moved towards the place where his rifle was hanging; " do you not know that it is very sinful to take a human life?"

" It is not sinful to take hers," he replied, calmly; "and so you would say if you knew—*what I won't tell you.* I care no more for shooting her than for shooting an old carrion-crow."

" But if you killed her it would be murder, and you would be hanged for it," urged Ellen, horrified at the callousness with which he contemplated so dreadful a deed.

"Oh, no !" he exclaimed, with a derisive laugh, " people are not hanged for murder in this house !"

" Not in this *house*, perhaps," said Ellen,

" but you would be taken away to a prison,
and then hanged with thousands of people
looking at you."

" I tell you, if any one in this house could
be hanged for murder, *she* would have been
hanged long ago!"

" Reginald!" said a deep voice, interrupting him in a tone of grave reproof.

Both turned, and saw Mr. Hawkshawe,
who had followed to apologise to Ellen as
soon as he could do so without exciting
his mother's irascible temper and insolent
remarks.

" Sir, I must leave your house immediately!" cried Ellen, forgetting all but Lady
Clarissa's insults.

" No, you must not," he replied, taking
her hand with an air of great kindness; " I
trust you feel convinced how deeply I regret
the annoyance to which you have been sub-
jected. I give you my word that it shall
never occur again. You shall take all your

meals with Reginald, and it will be your own fault if you ever again meet Lady Clarissa."

" I cannot stay," said Ellen, choking with resentful tears.

" Do you reflect upon what may be the consequence if you let her drive you away?" he demanded, with a glance towards the rifle. Ellen shuddered.

" If you *do* go away," said young Reginald, comprehending his father's hint, " I will shoot her, or kill her in some other way; but if you promise to stay, I will leave her alone."

" But it is not only on account of Lady Clarissa that I wish to go," said Ellen ; " I am much too young to be your teacher, Reginald. If you had had more experi· ence you would know that by remaining here with you I shall suffer greatly in the opinion of the world."

" Hang the world !" exclaimed Reginald,

impetuously; "I don't care for the world, and why should you care for it? Now, attend to what I say. And mind! I am a man, and I have strength and courage to do what I resolve to do, for I am not a peevish child, as my father wanted you to believe. I love you, and I will learn any-thing you like to teach me, and I will do whatever I can to please you, and make you happy, if you will stay. But if you go"——

He paused and drew a long breath, while his magnificent eyes were fixed on her with an expression that made her tremble. "If you go," he continued, in a terrible whisper, "I will burn the house down, and die among the ruins."

"This is a vain threat in your father's presence," said Ellen; "he has power to put you under restraint, and prevent such an act of guilty madness."

"Ask him if he has!" cried Reginald, exultingly.

"Ask me nothing, Miss Maynard," said Mr. Hawkshawe, as she turned an anxious frightened glance towards him, "and take nothing for granted as being possible or impossible. I entreat you to give heed to what Reginald has said, that he will learn from you willingly. And if that has no influence over you, I beg you to recollect the terms of your written agreement to remain as teacher to my son for one year. There is no mention of his age, so you cannot get free on that ground."

"No—it is impossible! I cannot remain!" cried Ellen, after a brief struggle with herself.

Those words to the wild soul of Reginald were like the spark that explodes a mine. At a bound he seized upon the loaded rifle, aimed it at Ellen's heart, and fired.

She fell to the ground with a faint cry, that seemed to be strangely echoed from the passage outside. After wounding her in the arm, the ball had passed through the door.

"Murderer! villain!" shouted Mr. Hawkshawe, springing like an enraged panther upon his son, and clutching him by the throat.

Reginald droppéd the gun and defended himself.

Well was it for Mr. Hawkshawe that Hector was not in the room, or the struggle would have been speedily decided against him. As it was, though he had the advantage of the first onset, and Reginald 'was bewildered and horror-stricken at the effect of his own mad action, he was by no means a match for the young savage. But before it could be decided by the strength of either party, the unnatural combat was interrupted by the innocent cause of it.

As she lay on the ground Ellen's consciousness began to return. At first she heard the sound of trampling feet, mixed with fierce though smothered imprecations.

She opened her eyes languidly, and to her horror beheld the father and son engaged in a mortal struggle. That sight recalled her senses in a moment. She rose up, not knowing that the blood was flowing fast from a wound in her arm, and tried to detach the young man's parricidal hands from his father's throat. Her strength alone could not have accomplished this, but her mere touch acted like magic. Reginald's arms dropped by his sides, but only to be raised again, and clasped round her in wild delight.

"I have not killed her!" he exclaimed; "I have not killed her! Forgive me! Will you forgive me? I did not mean to hurt you. I did not know what I was doing! Will you promise not to go away?"

"You take a strange means of making me stay," said Ellen, gently disengaging herself from his embrace; "but I will stay on one condition."

"What—what?" he demanded, eagerly.

"That you kneel and ask your father's forgiveness for having raised your hand against him," said Ellen.

"He struck me first," said Reginald, sullenly.

"That is no excuse," said Ellen; "for he is your father; and no act of his can justify you in striking him. Besides, think of the provocation."

"What was that to him?" said Reginald, turning pale with jealousy; "does he love you so much that he would kill his son for your sake?"

"He is responsible for my safety," she replied, "for he must have known that it was almost as dangerous to bring me here as to put me into the cage of an untamed lion. Nevertheless, I will brave the danger and stay with you, in the hope of making you a better——" she hesitated, not liking to acknowledge him to be a man, while to call him a boy would have been perfectly ludicrous; so she changed the form of her sentence, and added hastily, " of making you better, if you will apologize to your father, and give me your sacred promise never again, under whatever provocation, tolift your hand against him."

Reginald looked down. He was evidently moved by what she said, when a loud rap against the panel of the half-open door caused him to start, and the old fierce look came over his face.

" No," he said, through his clenched teeth, " I will not promise!"

" Reginald, I am hurt!" said Ellen, in a tremulous voice; " I feel very faint. Perhaps even yet I may die. But before my wound is seen to, I must hear you ask your father's pardon, and promise—and promise——"

Her voice faltered; she was nearly fainting.

Reginald cast a frightened glance upon

her, and threw himself at the feet of Mr.
Hawkshawe, who had sunk upon a chair
when his son released him, and was slowly
recovering from the effects of partial strangu-
lation.

" Father !" he cried, " I beg your forgiveness! And I swear by her blood," and he
held up his hand, which had come in contact with her wounded arm, " never again
to strike or injure you in any way, whatever you may do !"

Before Mr. Hawkshawe could distinctly
comprehend what all this meant—for that
his son should kneel to him for pardon
added much to the general confusion of his
senses, so improbable was it that such an
event could be anything but the disordered
imaginings of a weakened brain—Reginald
had sprung again to his feet, and caught
Ellen in his arms as she was falling.

" Father! father!" he shouted. " Call
some one to help her! She will die—she
will die !"

Mr. Hawkshawe staggered to the bell and rang it violently. Oliver, who had been alarmed by the report of the gun, answered the summons almost instantly, and when he rushed out again to call the housekeeper, according to his master's hurried orders, he encountered her at the door, for she too had been startled by the firing, and as she said, by a shrill scream that immediately followed it.

CHAPTER VIII.

A MYSTERIOUS VISITOR, AND A TALE OF HORROR.

ELLEN was laid upon the sofa, and Mr. Hawkshawe, Reginald, and Oliver retired, while Mrs. Sweetman, who possessed considerable skill in such matters, hastily examined the wound. The ball had passed through the arm, but fortunately without injuring bone or artery, though the wound bled profusely.

" She has fainted as much through fright as loss of blood," said the housekeeper, surveying Ellen's face more attentively than she had hitherto had leisure to do; " dear heart! but she's a pretty creature! Don't

you think so, sir?" she added, addressing
Mr. Hawkshawe, who, with the imperious
Reginald, she had permitted to return as
soon as the wound was dressed.

" Very," said Mr. Hawkshawe, laconically.

"Pretty!" repeated Reginald, in a tone
of contempt. "Why you call Nancy pretty.
Ellen is beautiful—she is magnificent! I
must learn names to call her by. All those
are too poor."

He said this in a low voice as he leant
over the couch, so that he was not heard by
the bystanders; but, as he concluded, Ellen
opened her eyes and looked at him. She
was still so faint that the idea of death was
uppermost in her mind. She saw the benevolent face of the housekeeper beside her;
and the figures of Mr. Hawkshawe and
Oliver in the rear were multiplied by her
uncertain vision into a crowd of strangers.

" He did not mean to kill me," said Ellen.
"I believe the gun went off by accident."

" You must not talk, Miss," said the housekeeper ; " drink this, and lie still."

Then turning to Mr. Hawkshawe, she added, " it will be best for her, sir, for everybody to leave the room but me. I'll stay by her."

Mr. Hawkshawe wished to stay, but could find no pretext for so doing. Oliver, of course, went without a word, excepting an assurance to Mrs. Sweetman that he would be on the alert to come at the gentlest ring of the bell.

Reginald, without troubling himself about excuses or pretexts, said flatly that he would not stir; so, partly from the habit of giving way to his moods, and partly from dread of an altercation which might alarm the invalid, he was suffered to remain.

Dark and tumultuous were the thoughts that chased each other through the chaotic mind of the young man, as he sat watching with steadfast eye the poor girl who had so nearly fallen a victim to his blind passions. And he could do nothing to soothe her while she lay there. Much as he loved music he could not play to her; he could not read; he could not converse so as to entertain her. All the strong feelings—the tenderness— the contrition—the agony of remorse—that consumed his soul, he must keep within, for he could find no words to express them.

He looked at the stains of blood upon his hands, and then at Ellen's wan face, and groaned aloud. She heard the groan, and held out her hand to him. In a moment he was kneeling by her side.

" I see," she murmured, " that you sin- cerely regret what you have done. Profit by the lesson, and curb your hasty temper for the future. Above all, show more deference towards your father. Remember the commandment, ' Honour thy father and thy mother.' "

" It was easy for you to keep that commandment," whispered Reginald, "for you have often told me how good and kind your father and mother always were to you. But mine!——"

"Repeat nothing to the discredit of your parents," interrupted Ellen; "*that* is not obeying the commandment. Your father, at least, is very kind to you."

"Oh yes, he is kind enough *now*," replied Reginald, carelessly; "but that is because all the others are gone. All his fine sons died, and then he was glad to take back the outcast. They all died," he continued, in a mysterious whisper, "after eating lozenges which their grandmother gave them. Just as they were growing up she became fond of them, and gave them lozenges; and then they died."

"Do not say such horrible things!" said Ellen. "Mrs. Sweetman said I must be quiet, and you are whispering insinuations dreadful enough to drive me into a fever."

"You may ask Mrs. Sweetman if it is not all true," he replied; "but I'll say no more about it. Do you really forgive me for firing at you? I did not know what I was doing; I only felt that I could not part from you, and that if I could not have you alive, I would have you dead."

"You were a reckless, hot-headed boy," said his monitress, trying to resume the tone of superiority with which she usually addressed him, and which, strange to say, she seemed to have lost when he shot her.

Reginald looked at a pier-glass that reflected his own figure, and that of his "governess;" and he smiled, as well he might.

Though on Ellen's first introduction, he was closely shaven, he had resolutely refused to perform that operation any more, and all the lower part of his face was consequently covered by a very thick, though short, black beard. His stature was almost gigantic, and his shoulders were broad and muscular. * His complexion, naturally very dark, was bronzed by exposure to the weather; for before the arrival of his gentle tutoress his principal occupation had been roaming about the hills and cliffs with his dogs and gun. Such was his own figure, as he saw it reflected in the glass.

Ellen, with her brown hair lying dishevelled upon the white pillow which had been brought for her accommodation, and pale from loss of blood, faintness, and agitation, looked very youthful and fragile. It was no wonder that Reginald smiled. She followed the direction of his eyes, and caught their glance of peculiar meaning.

"I will promise to be a good boy for the future," said he, in a tone of good-humoured mockery; "does not that," pointing to the glass, " look like the picture of a good little boy and his governess?"

"I know," said Ellen, reddening with

vexation, "that my position here is ridiculous, as well as annoying and dangerous; but it is not for you to remind me of it. If you hint at such a thing once more, I will not remain here a day longer."

"How!" said Reginald, with lowering brows; "have I not cured you of running away?"

"Say rather, have you not done your utmost to drive me away?" returned Ellen. "You seem to imagine that the same course of treatment which will subdue a horse or a dog may be adopted towards a rational being. But you will see your error if you persist in such conduct."

Here Mrs. Sweetman, who was sitting a little distance off, and by reason of a slight deafness had not heard a word of their conversation, which she wished for her patient's sake to interrupt, but dared not for fear of rousing Reginald's ungovernable temper, gave vent to her uneasiness in a suppressed

sigh, and "Oh dear! oh dear!" scarcely
audible. Ellen, however, heard it, and
taking the hint, said, "I am very weary,
and I think I can sleep, if you will go
away."

"I will be quiet," said Reginald, "but I
cannot go away."

He returned gently to his chair. Ellen
feigned sleep, until sleep really closed her
eyelids.

The two watchers remained motionless.
The hours stole away, and night settled
down around them. Once or twice the
door opened softly, and Mr. Hawkshawe
looked in; but at a sign from the housekeeper he withdrew.

Late in the evening Ellen awoke much
refreshed; the pain of the wound was considerably abated, and her mind had re·
covered from the excessive agitation undei
which she had suffered. Reginald, who
had remained so silent and motionless that

Mrs. Sweetman imagined that he too had been asleep, was immediately in full activity, and so tormented the invalid with his well-meant but unskilful assiduities, that she was fain to retire to the quiet of her own chamber.

The kind old housekeeper offered to sit up all night, but to this Ellen would not consent. Nevertheless as she had good reason to believe that it was her hopeful pupil's intention to take up his post outside her door, she willingly agreed that the old lady should occupy a temporary bed on a large sofa which formed part of the furniture of her chamber.

Though she had taken a draught composed of various herbs of a sedative nature, it was many hours before Ellen felt inclined to sleep. All the events of the last few months presented themselves vividly before her mind. The death of her father and mother; every incident of the funerals; the

genuine kindness of Mr. Smedley, contrasting so favourably with the malicious
triumph of those whose flatteries she had
treated with contempt in the time of her
prosperity. Then came the bitter recollection of Lady Willoughby's altered manner,
and the heart-sickness of hope deferred, for
not a word had she heard from Frank. It
was strange too that she had not received
an answer to either of the two letters that
she had written to the good doctor; one
immediately on her arrival at St. Osyth's
Priory, and another two months later.
Then she recalled Mr. Hawkshawe's evident
anxiety to prevent her knowing precisely
to what place he was taking her; and she
did him no great injustice by the suspicion
which flitted across her mind, that he might
perhaps have detained and destroyed her
letters. This it was quite possible for him
to do, as the letter-bag was always taken to
him to be locked before being dispatched to

the post-office. After dismissing the idea
again and again, as quite unworthy of one
who always behaved like a gentleman, she
resolved to write once more to Mr. Smedley,
detailing exactly how she was situated, and
giving as accurate a description as she could
of the most prominent features in the sur-
rounding country, lest the address mentioned to her by Mr. Hawkshawe should not
be sufficiently clear. This letter she intended
to drop in the village the next time she went
to church, in the hope that whoever found
it would put it into the post-office, which
she had been informed was near a mile
farther, though in which direction she had
never been able to discover, as the servants
could only enlighten her by mentioning the
names of places which she had never heard
of, and Mr. Hawkshawe purposely kept her
in the dark.

Why she intended giving such a pre-
cise description of her place of abode,

she did not give herself the trouble to consider. She could not suppose that Mr. Smedley would be knight-errant enough to leave his patients, and come there in search of her, and she *would* not suppose that he might impart the information to another, to whose soldierly character the knight-errantry would be quite suitable.

Having decided upon this matter for the future, Ellen began again to think of the past and the present. Mr. Hawkshawe's manners towards her had undergone a great, though gradual change. He had always been perfectly polite and deferential; but at first she had felt certain that he would have sacrificed her without hesitation, if he had deemed it necessary for the attainment of the grand object of his wishes, the training of his son, and fitting him to uphold the family honours. By slow degrees this impression wore off. His visits to the study, which used to be paid in the morning, and chiefly in order that he might watch over Reginald's progress, were now left till the evening, and assumed the appearance of being made to the teacher, rather than to the pupil.

This seemed natural enough, considering his passionate love for music, and Ellen was glad of it, for Mr. Hawkshawe's presence acted as a check upon her unruly pupil, who sometimes manifested so much fondness for his tutoress that she had great difficulty in restraining him at all within the bounds of decorum. He was too ignorant of the world and its rules to understand why he should not hold her hand in his, or put his arm round her waist, or lay his head on her lap or shoulder, when it did not inflict any pain upon her, and was very pleasant to himself. Yet, though he would not acknowledge that there was any wrong in attempting such familiarities, an

11—2

innate modesty made him desist from them
in the presence of a third party.

For this reason Ellen was pleased when
Mr. Hawkshawe began to spend his evenings with them, although she attributed it
to a suspicion on his part that the poor
teacher had designs upon the hand and
fortune of her wealthy pupil.

She smiled haughtily at the idea, and
thought of Frank Willoughby.

After a while a feeling of jealousy began
to develope itself between the father and
son, and the attentions of the former
became so marked, that Ellen often wished
that she had only the unsophisticated and
innocent Reginald to deal with.

She would have been contented to play
to them all the evening, especially as,
under the pretext that it made her nervous
if any one looked over her, she had
succeeded in establishing it as a rule that
neither of them was to turn over the leaves

for her, but both were to remain at a sufficient distance.

But fond as they both were of music, it did not always suit them.

Mr. Hawkshawe was very fond of chess, and Ellen was a good player; consequently Reginald wished to learn, and sat close beside her to watch the game. This did well enough for a time, till lowering looks and angry words began to show that fresh jealousies were arising; and her position, as at once the cause of contention and the medium of peace, became more and more arduous and embarrassing. It was with great difficulty that she had kept her pupil and his father from an open rupture, and the catastrophe of that day was only the bursting of a storm that had long been threatening.

She wished very much that she could escape from her engagement; but the penalty, which she never dreamt of eluding

by any subtlety of the law, would have
swallowed up nearly the whole of her
worldly possessions. Another and stronger
reason for remaining was that she had acquired considerable power over Reginald's
mind, and was rapidly drawing him into a
love of learning for its own sake, which
would make him willing, after a time,
to receive instruction from more fitting
tutors.

On one subject alone his mind seemed
incapable of receiving any impression. He
could not, or would not, entertain a religious idea. Ellen often prayed fervently
for strength and guidance to overcome this
difficulty. She blamed herself for want of
zeal in the work that had been appointed
her of leading an erring and benighted soul
into the way of salvation. And now, while
she lay awake with the pain of her wound,
she recalled many opportunities that she had
omitted, when a word in season might have

been spoken; and almost believed that the danger she had incurred, and the wound she had received, were a direct punishment for her lukewarmness.

As she lay in a half-waking, half-dreaming state, she imagined that she saw a face looking steadfastly at her, through the partially-opened curtains. Probably the opiate which she had swallowed aided in some degree the slight delirium under which she laboured, and caused this delusion. There was a wood fire blazing brightly on the hearth, but the light was intercepted by the large sofa on which Mrs. Sweetman lay, as well as by the thick dark curtains of the bed, so that the side on which the face appeared was thrown into deep shadow. At first it struck her as bearing so strong a resemblance to Reginald that Ellen imagined that her pupil had stolen in to see if she were sleeping; but a sudden gleam of the flickering light showed

her that it was the countenance of a
woman.

The complexion was swarthy—the eyes
large, black, and lustrous, and the whole
appearance was that of an extremely handsome gipsy; not young, yet preserving the
beauty which in general disappears before
middle age in that hardy race. As she
gazed, the resemblance to Reginald became
more and more striking, until she began to
fancy that the apparition must be the mere
"coinage of her brain," which pertinaciously
recalled the face of her pupil as she had
seen him before his beard had grown. She
passed her hand across her eyes to clear her
vision, and when she looked again the space
between the curtains was vacant. Satisfied
that it was a mere optical delusion she tried
to compose herself to sleep, when the sudden
appearance of Mrs. Sweetman at the other
side of the bed again aroused her.

" Is anything amiss ?" asked Ellen.

" No, Miss," replied the old woman,
" only I thought you were out of bed and
moving about the room. I really thought
I saw you, but I suppose hearing you move
made me fancy that."

" I have not stirred," said Ellen; " perhaps it was a cat. Look round the room,
will you, and send her out."

Mrs. Sweetman looked under the bed, and
in every corner where a cat could by any
possibility be concealed; and as nothing was
discovered Ellen felt satisfied that no human intruder could have been in the room.
As she wished to know whether the door
was locked, and at the same time to avoid
frightening the old lady, she suggested that
the cat might have been scratching at the
door. The peculiar click as the key turned
in the lock convinced her that it had been
secured; and therefore if her nocturnal
visitant had been a creature of flesh and
blood, she could not have made her exit in

the usual way. The housekeeper's exclamation as she looked into the passage also
suggested an easy explanation of the noise
which the old lady had heard.

" La! Master Reginald!" she said, "how
you did frighten me!"

" Is Mr. Reginald there?" asked Ellen.

" Yes, Miss, lying across the door-way, as
if he was asleep."

" I am not asleep," he said, in a low voice.

" Reginald! come here!" said Ellen,
much to Mrs. Sweetman's astonishment, as
well as to the startling of all her notions
of propriety. The young man had no
such ideas, but sprang across the room, and
knelt by the bedside.

" Do you wish to make me very ill?"
asked Ellen.

" You know I do not," he replied, in a
hoarse whisper; " you know I would die to
serve you, now that I am in my senses."

" Then go to your own room," said Ellen,
" and pray for God's help that you may re-

pent sincerely of the crimes you have attempted to commit."

" I do repent," he said, taking her hand,
and passing it across his face that she might
feel the tears with which his cheeks and
beard were wet.

" I do not doubt that you repent in your
own rough way," said Ellen ; " but such
repentance is not sufficient before God.
Go!" she said, and she fervently pressed his
hand, for he had not suffered her to with-
draw hers, " go and humble yourself at the
Throne of Grace, and pray that this occasion, which might have ended so fatally
for you, may be turned, by the help of
Divine Wisdom, into the means of your
salvation."

" This occasion, as you call it, might
have been much worse for you than for
me!" he said, with a shudder.

" Nay, not so," she replied, " for I am
somewhat prepared, and should not fear to
meet my Maker; but what would have

been your state, with the blood of a fellow-creature on your hands!—Perhaps even with your father's life to answer for!"

"That state should not have lasted long," he said, smiling grimly.

"Oh! worse and worse!" she cried, rightly divining his meaning. "What then would have been your fate, hurried by your own act into eternity!"

"Do all people who have committed murder go down to that bottomless pit you have told me of, and remain there for ever?" he asked.

"We are taught to believe that such will be their fate, unless they repent," replied Ellen.

"Then I don't wish to go there at all," said Reginald; "because I should always see my grandmother, for she will never repent. But as you are sure to go to Heaven, I should like to go there too. Tell me what I must do!"

Ellen sighed heavily, as she thought how unsuitable was such a state of mind for the momentous task which he undertook with so much levity.

"First," said she, "you must pray with all your heart and soul for Divine grace to assist you and enlighten you. Then you must learn God's commandments, and endeavour to keep them. I can talk no more, Reginald; I am weak and weary. Good night."

He kissed her hand, and went softly out of the room. In another minute the door of his own room was heard to shut; the sound reverberated through the vaulted passage, and all was still.

"I never saw any one so changed in all my born days as Mr. Reginald is since you've been here, Miss," said Mrs. Sweetman, turning the key and approaching the bed; "before you came his temper was awful!"

"I have good cause to know that it is still

rather ungovernable," said Ellen, glancing at her wounded arm. "How is it that his education has been so sadly neglected?"

"I hardly know the rights of the story, Miss," replied the housekeeper, "for I have not lived in the family much above six year. If there's anybody besides the family themselves that really does know, it is old Oliver; but he is so close one can get nothing out of him. What I have heard is as this: master married on the sly when he was very young, and he put his wife to school somewhere near London, because she was a foreigner, and had been taught very little. He said she was a foreigner, but many people that live about here, and saw her often, have told me that she was as like a gipsy as anybody could be. After a time he brought her home, and then it seems that her temper was that dreadful that he had a miserable life of it. However, she brought him a son, and that was a comfort to him, and the child seemed to smooth her humours too, and so they got on very well for a few years. But then Lady Clarissa grew tired of living in Paris, and came to reside here. After that, there was no peace in the house for anybody. Her ladyship never goes into a passion nor quarrels herself, but she has the cleverest way of setting other people by the ears that ever I heard of. She never seems so pleased as when she has made two people disagree and quarrel, and it was easy enough to do it here; for master is hot-tempered, and Mrs. Hawkshawe, they say, had the spirit of Lucifer when she was roused. When Master Reginald was about four years old they had a terrible quarrel, and Mrs. Hawkshawe swore by a number of strange outlandish names, that she would be revenged. That night she and the child both disappeared; and it was fully believed all round the country that she had jumped with him into the sea.

And so, after a while, it was all forgotten;
and then there was a talk of Mr. Hawkshawe's marrying again, but Lady Clarissa
did all she could to prevent it, because she
hated the family to which the young lady
belonged. However, Mr. Hawkshawe would
not be hindered, and so he appointed a suite
of rooms for his mother, with her own carriage and servants, that she need never
meet his wife anywhere about the house,
and then he went to London, and married
Miss Merryweather, notwithstanding she
was the daughter of a manufacturer. She
had a very large fortune, but, poor thing!
she had not much enjoyment of it. In six
years she had three fine boys, and they all
had the fair hair and fresh rosy complexion
of their mother's family. However, their
father loved them, and was as proud of
them as he had been of his eldest boy, who
is every bit a Hawkshawe, with his large
black eyes, and jet black hair. As for Lady

Clarissa, she went on worse than ever. A few days after each baby was born, she had it brought to her, and took a good look at it; and when she saw the poor little innocent's sweet blue eyes and flaxen hair, she scowled at it as if it was a toad or a viper, and sent it away again. And the nurse that carried the youngest told me on her death-bed, that Lady Clarissa, as she looked at the blessed infant, muttered to herself, 'They're none of them Hawkshawes! But she shall repent it!' The nurse durstn't for her life repeat those words to anybody at the time, but things that transpired afterwards caused them to play upon her mind to that degree, that she could not die easy till she had confided them to some one, and so she told me."

"What was it that gave Lady Clarissa's words so much importance?" asked Ellen, with painful interest; for many points of the story tallied strangely with the hints thrown out by Reginald respecting the character of his grandmother, and the fate of his brothers.

"It was this," replied Mrs. Sweetman, dropping her voice to a still lower key; "just as the eldest boy was growing up to manhood, and his father and mother were rejoicing over his growth and cleverness, for he had been to the best school in England, and Mr. Hawkshawe was talking of sending him to Oxford in another year, all at once Lady Clarissa seemed to take a great liking for him, and she began to dine with the rest of the family, and to spend her evenings with them. Mr. Hawkshawe was delighted, and his poor wife no doubt was pleased to see that she was no longer a bar between her husband and his mother, though she never seemed able to conquer her fear of the awful old lady. Well, one night everybody in the house heard the Death Wail; that is, as perhaps you've heard, Miss, some strange music that is

always heard before the death of any of
the Hawkshawe family. The next day the
poor boy had a slight cough, and her ladyship gave him some lozenges that she always
carried in her pocket for her own cough.
It has been whispered, though I don't know
who the story began with, that she put *one*
into his mouth, which was different from
the rest, and that she took it out of a little
gold box. However that may be, he was
seized with terrible convulsions, and died
that very night. The doctor said something
about poison, and Lady Clarissa instantly
made a great fuss about her lozenges, and
sent some to a great chemist in London to
be examined; but of course *they* were all
right; and so the matter was dropped, for
those who had suspicions were too much
afraid to breathe a word about them. But
the mourning for the eldest son was not over
when the Death Wail was heard again louder
than before, and the other two boys were

12—2

seized in the same way, and died within an
hour of each other. It was said that these
fits were common in their mother's family.
Mr. Hawkshawe had their bodies opened,
but no poison could be found, and so
the poor lambs were buried beside their
brother. Lady Clarissa seemed quite overpowered with grief, and went into the
deepest mourning.

"Well, Miss," continued the housekeeper, "you'd think all this was horrors
enough for one family; but stranger things
yet was to come. The night after the
funeral of the two boys the whole house
was roused by the most fearful shrieks that
mortal ears ever heard. All the servants
rushed in alarm to Mrs. Hawkshawe's room,
from which the cries proceeded. But Lady
Clarissa and Mr. Hawkshawe, who had
been sitting with his mother in her dressing
room, were there first, all except Oliver.
He was just going up to bed, after seeing

to the fastenings of the doors, and the safety
of the house, when he heard the screams,
and run into the room without a moment's
hesitation, because he thought his lady must
be on fire. What he saw there he has never,
to my knowledge, revealed to anybody.
Perhaps his life might not be worth much
if he did. However, Mr. Hawkshawe and
her ladyship sent all the servants out of the
room; and as Oliver passed among them
without seeming to see any of them, and
looking as white as this counterpane, he
muttered, ' I saw them all—all three! all
poi——' or some word that began with a
p, and then he gasped, and hurried away
from his fellow-servants; and though they
followed, and asked him what he had seen,
he would not utter another word, but locked
himself into his room. All the rest were too
frightened to go to bed. Besides, poor
Mrs. Hawkshawe continued screaming all
through that dreary night. The house-

keeper—it was before I came, you know,
Miss—went up and asked if she might send
one of the men-servants for the doctor; but
Mr. Hawkshawe was in such a rage with
her for interfering, and looked so awful,
that she durstn't for her life go near him
again. Two of the men went up to Oliver's
door several times, and still his light was
burning, and they heard his voice, as if he
was praying, which no doubt he was. You
may be sure the servants were all frightened
enough, for when they came to compare
notes, and some told what they had heard
Oliver say, and some said they had heard
Mrs. Hawkshawe say in the midst of her
screams, 'my children,' and some 'poison,'
and others different words that all seemed
to show that something dreadful had happened, they all believed that the spirits of
the three boys had appeared to their mother,
and that Oliver, running in first, had seen
them too. What made them believe this

all the more was that when he came down in the morning his hair was white as snow. The day before, he was a fresh-coloured, cheerful sort of man, with jet black hair; but from that time no one ever saw a trace of colour on his cheeks, or a smile on his face, and his hair was that morning just what you see it now."

" And what more happened to Mrs. Hawkshawe?" asked Ellen, whose sympathies were aroused by the sorrows of that patient, timorous woman.

" She left off screaming after that night," replied Mrs. Sweetman, " but her senses were gone, and she has ever since been in the state she is in now. A great change came over Mr. Hawkshawe too; he became gloomy and silent, and looked ten years older. He had used to like company and gaiety, but after the death of his sons, and his poor wife's heavy affliction, he gave up society altogether, and scarcely ever saw anybody.

His only amusement was going out alone
with his gun among the hills, and once, it
was about two years ago, he met with a
youth so like his lost child, Reginald, that
he brought him home with him; and sure
enough when they examined his left arm
they found a natural mark which they knew
him by, as well as the letters R. H., for
Reginald Hawkshawe, which his mother
had had a fancy to tattoo by the side of it.
One would have thought the poor gentleman would have taken leave of his senses
with joy at recovering his son; but his
pleasure was soon checked, when he found
out how terribly ignorant the boy was. If
you'll believe me, Miss, he could scarcely so
much as talk, and he did not know the
names of the commonest things about the
house. In fact he was just as if he had been
brought up in a cave by some wild beast.
He could not tell where he had lived, nor
who he had lived with.   At first   my

master had the clergyman to come and teach him, but that wouldn't do. He would not learn from him, and he put himself into such dreadful passions that Mr. Gibson was afraid to come near him again. Then his father observed that he picked up words fast enough from the maid servants, so he engaged Miss Gibson, the curate's sister, to come every morning and instruct him; but the obstinate boy had taken such a violent hatred to his grandmother, that he could not bear the sight of an elderly woman, and poor Miss Gibson ran away after a five minutes' trial, almost scared out of her wits. After that he tried a young gentleman, but he could do no good; Mr. Reginald seemed jealous that any one so near his own age should be so much wiser than himself. Then my master went off to London and fetched you, Miss; and, dear me! how he has improved since!"

"And you really believe," said Ellen,

musingly, "that the spirits of those three poor boys appeared to their mother, and gave her an intimation of the cause of their death?"

"Indeed I do, Miss, as firmly as I believe in anything."

"Have they been seen again?" asked Ellen.

"*Something* has been seen, more than once," said Mrs. Sweetman, "and it is so well known, that there is not one of the servants besides Oliver who will go about the house alone after nightfall."

"But if Oliver really beheld, or even believed he beheld the apparitions in Mrs. Hawkshawe's room, one would suppose that he would be the most timid of all, because he would feel sure there were such things, and would fear to see them again," said Ellen.

"Oliver is prepared, Miss," replied the housekeeper, solemnly; " at every spare moment he is reading his Bible, and we all think he spends half the night in prayer."

"It is a terrible tale," said Ellen, "and full of mystery; but let us hope that the darker part of it—the poisoning of all those boys by their own grandmother—is not true. If it were, surely some notice would have been taken of it."

"Why, you see, Miss, the bodies were examined by Mr. Hawkshawe's own wish, and nothing was found; and after the fright that drove his poor wife out of her mind, even if he knew or suspected how they came by their death, he could not accuse his own mother. And yet if he *did* know it, that would account for the change in his behaviour."

"It is too dreadful to dwell upon," said Ellen, with a shudder. "Tell me something else before I go to sleep, or those poor boys and that terrible old lady will be in my dreams all night. Are there no other ghosts about the house? Has not the first Mrs. Hawkshawe been seen by any one?"

" Oh dear yes!" replied Mrs. Sweetman, "she has been often seen."

" I thought so," said Ellen; "and did no one suspect that she might be still alive?"

" She alive! La, no!" exclaimed Mrs. Sweetman; "where could she have been hidden all these years?"

" Where was Reginald hidden?" said Ellen, "and who could have brought him up as though he had been nurtured in the cave of a wild beast? Who but a woman who was maddened by real or imaginary wrongs, and who took the sharpest vengeance in sending back a young savage to claim the family honours?"

" Then perhaps it was she who poisoned the children by the second wife," said Mrs. Sweetman; " she might want to get them out of the way."

" No, no," replied Ellen; "if they died

by poison, it was not given by *her* hand. They could not interfere with her son's rights, for they were illegitimate, and could not claim even the younger brother's portion. Is there a portrait of her in the house?" she asked, after a thoughtful pause.

"Oh yes! there's a large full-length picture of her in her riding habit, leaning upon her favourite horse," said Mrs. Sweetman; "it used to hang in the dining-room; but after she went away it was put into another room that is never used. I'll show it you when you get about again. It is in the room next to this."

"Thank you, Mrs. Sweetman," said Ellen, drowsily. "I think I can sleep now."

The housekeeper watched the heavy eyelids close over the soft grey eyes, and then stole gently back to her own bed.

CHAPTER IX.

THE DEATH WAIL.

THE following morning Ellen awoke to a strange sense of confusion, amid which the only permanent and real thing seemed to be that she was suffering acute pain in her wounded arm.

All else was vague and fleeting. She could not recollect who had wounded her; but as she dozed, or became partially insensible, the strangest ideas upon this point chased each other through her brain. Sometimes she fancied that Lady Clarissa had bitten her; sometimes that Mr. Hawkshawe had shot her for attempting to escape;

sometimes that the strange dark woman who had peered at her through the bed-curtains was hanging her by a hook through the arm because she refused to eat a lozenge taken out of a little gold box.

" I will not have it!—It is poison!" she exclaimed, dashing out her hand with violence.

A crash of glass followed, and a muttered ejaculation from Mrs. Sweetman; and Ellen opened her eyes to find that in her half-delirious sleep she had flung down a glass of cooling drink which the good house-keeper, seeing her feverish and restless state, was holding to her lips, and trying to induce her to drink. She laughed faintly at her blunder, and drank another glass of the anti-febrile decoction, after which she again sank into a troubled sleep.

A short time afterwards Mr. Hawkshawe tapped softly at the door to inquire how she was progressing. Mrs. Sweetman allowed him to approach the bed, that he might judge for himself. He stood at the foot, and gazed long and earnestly at the sleeping girl.

" Don't you think the doctor ought to be sent for, sir?" whispered the housekeeper.

"Not if your skill will suffice, my good lady," he replied. " I wish above all things, as I told you last night, to avoid having this sad accident known. Nevertheless, a horse shall be kept saddled that Dr. Welsh may be sent for at any moment of the day or night, if you see symptoms of danger."

At this moment Ellen opened her eyes, and fixed them intently upon Mr. Hawkshawe. She did not appear to recognise him, and her eyes wandered away and remained for some minutes riveted as upon some object at his right hand.

" There they are, standing beside you !" she said, in a low clear voice, extending her unwounded arm in the same direction ; " all

three of them!—Golden-haired boys, beautiful as angels!—All poisoned!"

Her arm·dropped, and her eyes closed
again in deep slumber. Mr. Hawkshawe
shuddered violently, and hurried out of the
room without uttering a word.

Mrs. Sweetman was awe-struck. She
fully believed that Ellen had actually beheld the apparitions of the three murdered
boys (forgetting the more probable solution
of the mystery—that the vision was only
the creation of a disordered brain, stimulated
by her own recital of the previous night),
and though she knew that such innocent
souls must be harmless, yet the dread of en-
countering any supernatural visitant so
overcame her that she sank upon her knees,
hid her face in the bedclothes, and prayed
aloud.

A touch on the shoulder startled her.
She looked round, almost expecting to see
three youthful figures in white garments;

but there was only one, and that was clothed in black.

"Oliver!" she exclaimed, rising from her knees, and trembling from head to foot,— "O dear, how you frightened me!"

"You were frightened enough before, Mrs. Sweetman," he replied, in a subdued tone; "how is it? Have you seen them?"

"No, thank Heaven! *I* have not," she replied; "but *she* saw them. She said they were standing there, by master's side. And then he rushed out like a madman."

"As well he might," said the old man, with a sigh; "and yet, poor gentleman! he is guiltless of any wrong to them. No doubt she did see them. They cannot rest."

"Those are awful words, Oliver," said Mrs. Sweetman, in a terrified whisper; "do you mean to say that you know how the poor boys died? Many folks say you do."

"I say nothing, missis, and never shall, unless a great alteration takes place," replied the old man; " and I advise you not to trust too much to what the gossips tell you. Nobody *can* know the truth. But I'm forgetting the errand I came for. Mr. Hawkshawe wishes to know how the young lady is, and whether her nerves are shaken at all."

" Tell him she has not opened her eyes since he was here," said Mrs. Sweetman, " and that she is in a calm sleep, from which I hope she will awake much better."

Oliver went out with his noiseless step. Mrs. Sweetman deputed one of the maids to watch quietly in Ellen's apartment during her absence, and descended to the kitchen to attend to her domestic concerns, bidding her deputy ring the bell in case the patient awoke, or appeared restless. In about an hour she returned, and found that Ellen was still locked in that deep healing slumber.

" And no wonder," observed the girl

who had been left to watch her (I shall not venture to transcribe her Cornish dialect); " for somebody has been playing such lovely music, it 'most sent me to sleep too."

" Playing music!" said the housekeeper, in amazement. " Who can have been playing music? Was it Master Reginald?"

" Oh no, I see him walking about in the garden all the time," said the girl.

"Who could it have been?" said Mrs. Sweetman. " What sort of music was it ? Was it like a pianna?"

"No—not a bit like a pianna," replied the girl. " It was more like the organ at church when it plays very soft and sweet, and like women's voices, you know. I dare say if you sit quiet a bit you'll hear it."

They sat still, listening, and presently their ears were greeted by a strain of soft wild music like the solemn breathings of the wind over an Eolian harp.

" The Lord have mercy upon us !" ex-

claimed the housekeeper. "There!—go
down, Grace, go down; and don't you say
a word about this music to anybody. It's
the death warning of the family. Who is
it to be, I wonder?"

"Is it for Miss Maynard?" whispered
Grace, turning pale, and trembling like an
aspen leaf.

"No—it would not play for her, because
she is not one of the family," said Mrs.
Sweetman. "It must be a Hawkshawe,
either by birth or marriage. Pray Heaven
it may be the old lady! Now mind you
don't mention it," she repeated, seeing that
the girl was very anxious to get out of the
haunted room, adding, with a stroke of
policy to enforce the performance of her
request, "it always brings ill luck upon the
first person who speaks about it."

"Oh no! I won't say a word," said
Grace, clutching at the door handle; "only
pray don't set me to watch here again,

please. I don't like it at all." And she beat a hasty retreat.

Probably Mrs. Sweetman relished the lonely watch as little as her deputy. She was, at least, very glad when Ellen awoke, and asked for something to eat. She was, as her good nurse had predicted, considerably better after her long sleep.

"I hope you were not disturbed, Miss," said the housekeeper, anxious to know whether she had heard the music.

"Oh no, quite the contrary, if you can understand how that may be," replied Ellen, smiling; "for I was just awaking when that Eolian harp began to play, and it sent me to sleep again. Where is it?"

"Where is what, Miss?" asked Mrs. Sweetman, in a state of utter bewilderment.

"Why, that Eolian harp that has been playing so sweetly," said Ellen; "surely you must have heard the music?"

"Oh! yes, Miss, I heard some music,"

replied Mrs. Sweetman; "but I don't know where it came from, nor who played it."

"I know the sound of that music well," said the patient; "it is not any *person* who plays it." (Mrs. Sweetman shuddered.) "It is an instrument with strings, that is placed in an open window; and when the wind blows through it, it produces that beautiful wild music that you heard. It must have been fixed up this morning, or I should have heard it before. No doubt that strange youth, Reginald, being unable yet to play well enough to please me, has placed this 'harp of the winds' somewhere near, that its wild tones may lull me to rest."

"I dare say he has, Miss," said Mrs. Sweetman, to whom, however, Ellen's last remarks had been only half addressed. Her belief in the supernatural origin of the sounds she had heard remained, nevertheless, as firm as ever.

Anxious to prevent any further inquiries on this subject, which might lead to discoveries dangerously agitating and alarming to her patient, Mrs. Sweetman commenced her preparations for dressing the wound. It was progressing favourably; but the doctoress thought it advisable that Ellen should remain in bed, on low diet, for that day at least.

Many were the anxious inquiries made at the door during the day by Mr. Hawkshawe and Reginald, but the former did not again request leave to enter the room, and the latter was of course rigorously excluded.

The music was not heard again, and the housekeeper went to bed, in the hope that it might not be repeated.

Ellen had frequently thought of it, and wished she might hear again the wild, soothing, dream-like tones. By some untraceable chain of imagination she had linked the music with the mysterious face that had looked through her curtains the night before; and now, as her eyes were closing, she opened them again to see if the swarthy countenance was at its post. The space was vacant. Only the fire-light danced upon a large old wardrobe that stood against the wall. Her eyes closed fast, and she was dreaming that the Eolian melody was murmuring in her ear, when its tones swept so loud and so near that they awoke her with a start.

The harp, if harp it were, seemed to be actually in the room; then it sank away, and moaned outside the windows. Again it passed along the lofty ceiling, and then died away in mournful wailings through the long, echoing corridors.

She raised her head and listened. A slight motion of the curtains caught her eye. There was the gipsy-like face again, but so changed, so haggard, so full of pain,

so death-like, that she could hardly recognise it.

"Oh, heavens! She is dying! Help!
help!" cried Ellen, with a shriek of terror,
at the same time falling back, fainting.

Aroused by the cry, Mrs. Sweetman
rushed to her assistance. For a long time
the fainting fit refused to yield to the restoratives which she brought; and she began
to wonder whether the warning could have
been intended for the young lady, though a
stranger to the family.

Mingled with much real sorrow at the
probable death of her fair patient, came
sundry misgivings concerning the consequences to herself, if a coroner's jury should
return a verdict of culpable negligence in
undertaking the cure of a gun-shot wound,
without calling in the aid of a regular
practitioner.

At length, to her great joy, the poor girl
gave signs of returning consciousness. She

pressed her hand to her forehead, looked hurriedly round, and then seemed by a sudden effort to recollect all.

" See to her!" she said, pointing towards the farther side of the bed, where the face had appeared. " Has she fallen on the ground? Is she lying there now? Oh! see to her! Never mind me—I am quite well now."

" Who are you talking about, Miss?" demanded the bewildered housekeeper; " there is nobody here. You must keep quiet, and not give way to these fancies."

" It was no fancy," replied Ellen, earnestly. " I saw the face as plainly as I now see yours; and death was written upon it. It was—I am sure it was—the face of the first Mrs. Hawkshawe—of Reginald's mother."

" The Lord preserve us!" cried Mrs. Sweetman; " she's seen a ghost!"

" No—it was not a ghost," said Ellen; " it

was a living, or rather a dying woman. I
recollect now that as I fell, when that madman fired, I heard a scream from the other
side of the door, and afterwards there was
a knock against it, which was evidently a
signal to Reginald. She must have been
outside the door, and the shot, after passing
through my arm, went through the panel,
and struck her. Oh, heaven! are the
crimes and miseries of this unhappy family
to have no end? That wretched youth has
destroyed his own mother! I feel convinced it is she; but I must see her portrait, and have positive proof of it before I
speak to Reginald."

"Oh, dear! she is quite beside herself!"
cried the old lady, vainly endeavouring to
keep Ellen from jumping out of bed;
"she'll go and catch her death, and I can't
hold her."

"I am not delirious, Mrs. Sweetman,"
said Ellen, as calmly as her anxiety would

allow. "I shall run but slight risk if I wrap up well, and am careful; and what is that, when a fellow-creature is suffering, and dying within our reach, with perhaps no one to succour her, or breathe one word of hope or comfort to her departing soul?"

"But, my sweet young lady!" remonstrated the housekeeper, "the door is fast locked, so how could anybody have got in?"

"I shall not stop to inquire how," replied Ellen. "I only know that she was here. Do you not remember the noise you heard last night, when you thought I was walking about the room? She was here then, but I did not tell you, lest you should be frightened, and I thought it might be only my own imagination when I saw her face looking through the curtains. Help me on with my dressing-gown. It is useless to try to prevent my going."

Convinced at last that it was useless, yet

still inclined to remonstrate, Mrs. Sweetman did as she was bid, and Ellen was soon
enveloped in as many wrappers as she
could bear the weight of.

"Now," said she, "show me the picture."

"Oh, dear! dear! How shall I answer
for it to Mr. Hawkshawe if you go and kill
yourself?" cried the perplexed housekeeper.

"I shall not die before I have time to
exculpate you entirely," said Ellen, scarcely
able to repress a smile; "but I assure you
I run very little danger if you will guide
me at once to the picture. If I have to
run about the house seeking for it, it may
do me great harm."

"But where's the use of your going now
to look at that picture, Miss?" said Mrs.
Sweetman. "Why not stay till to-morrow?
The picture won't run away."

"But the woman may die," replied Ellen.
"If she be Mrs. Hawkshawe, depend upon it
Reginald knows where to find her. And

in one word, Mrs. Sweetman, if you do not instantly lead the way to this picture, I shall seek for it myself."

With a deep groan, Mrs. Sweetman thereupon took up the candle, and walked out into the lobby, followed by the impatient Ellen.

CHAPTER X.

WHY THE DEATH WAIL WAS HEARD.

MRS. SWEETMAN conducted Ellen into the lobby, and then entered the room immediately on their left.

It was a large apartment, similar to that which Ellen occupied, except that the furniture was older, and looked quite neglected, and that it had the mouldy, damp smell usual in rooms that have been long closed.

A large picture stood by the wall, and towards this the two visitors advanced.

"Here it is," said the housekeeper, holding up the light.

It was a full-length portrait of a beautiful

brunette, dressed in riding costume, and with one hand resting on the mane of a magnificent horse.

"It is the same," said Ellen, after an earnest perusal of the face; "that countenance is too remarkable to be mistaken. Go now, Mrs. Sweetman, as quickly as possible, and call Reginald. Tell him to come to me instantly. I will sit by the fire, and keep myself very quiet, while you are gone."

With a smothered exclamation expressive of vain remonstrance, Mrs. Sweetman, after assisting her patient to return to her room, went on her errand, while Ellen sat thinking over her plans.

The first step certainly was to obtain from Reginald all the information possible respecting his mother; and that information must guide her future conduct. The recollection of that haggard and pain-stricken face dwelt upon her mind, and she felt impatient of the housekeeper's prolonged absence, and fancied every moment that she sat inactive was a crime against humanity. At length the door opened.

"Shall Mr. Reginald come in, Miss?" asked Mrs. Sweetman.

"Yes—yes," cried Ellen, starting up, and advancing with her hand raised and extended with a gesture of adjuration. "Oh, Reginald, do not imagine that I desire to pry into the secrets of your family; but tell me truly, is your mother alive?"

Reginald's fine eyes were cast down; he appeared much confused, and made no reply.

"Answer me, answer me!" she entreated, placing her hand upon his with a gentle pressure, for she knew by experience, that the touch of that soft white hand was a talisman to control him in his most wilful moods.

The charm failed now for the first time. He pressed her hand to his lips, and held it between his own, while he looked at her seriously, and replied, with a grave dignity

which she had never before observed in him,
"Ellen, I have always felt you to be my
superior in everything but brute strength,
and the power of loving intensely. I have
not been too proud to acknowledge your
superiority, and I have profited more by
your instructions than perhaps you have
imagined. One of your strongest precepts
has been 'keep a promise sacred.' You
now demand, with those passionate eyes
fixed upon mine, that I shall break a promise solemnly pledged. Not even for *you*
will I break my word."

He dropped her hand, and turned away.
Ellen was astounded. Where or how, she
thought, had he suddenly acquired a command of language to which he had never
before been able to attain? And whence
came that decided and manly bearing? She
felt that he was her pupil no longer.

"Last night," she said, "a face looked at
me through my curtains. It was the face

of a dark-complexioned woman, bearing a
striking resemblance to yourself. To-night
I saw the same countenance again, but so
distorted by suffering that I know she is very
ill. I have seen the portrait of your mother,
and by that means I know that it is she."

The young man uttered a cry of anguish
and darted from the room.

In a few minutes he returned, and summoned both Ellen and the housekeeper to
follow him. He led them into the room
which they had before visited, and drawing
aside the curtains which had concealed her
from their sight on the former occasion, he
disclosed the figure of a woman, writhing
with pain, though uttering no groan.

" It *is* Mrs. Hawkshawe!" exclaimed
Mrs. Sweetman, glancing from the living
woman to the portrait, and back again.

" It is," repeated Reginald, in a low voice
to Ellen. " Can you tell what is the matter
with her?"

"It is useless to try to cure me," said the sufferer. "I know I am dying. I did not feel it much at first, but it is killing me now."

"What is it, mother? What do you say is killing you?" demanded Reginald, fondly.

"You could not help it," she said, gazing at him with filmy eyes. "You did not know I was behind the door, and the ball went through and struck me. But it was not your fault, my own loved boy!"

"*I!*" shrieked Reginald, in a frenzy—"*I* shoot you! Mother, mother! unsay those words! Do not drive me mad by telling me *I* have killed you!"

"'Tis a just punishment," she said. "I brought you up like a savage to revenge myself on your father, and the consequence of my folly and wickedness has fallen upon myself. I am justly punished."

"But the blow should not have come from *my* hand," whispered Reginald, in a voice choking with grief.

"Do not grieve so much about it, my son," said the invalid. "It was an accident, and we must all die at last."

"Are you prepared for death?" asked Ellen. "Will you not see the clergyman?"

"Had I not better send for the doctor?" suggested Mrs. Sweetman. "She may not be so bad as she thinks."

"No, no," cried the dying woman, impatiently, and endeavouring to raise herself from the bed; "I shall be dead before he can get here. Neither doctor nor clergyman. You shall pray for me, Ellen Maynard, when I have spoken of some worldly concerns. Your prayers, that come fresh from the heart, are better than those a priest says by rote."

"Do you wish Mr. Hawkshawe to be called?" asked Ellen.

"No," she replied, quickly. "He has long believed me dead; let him think so still."

"Let me send for him," said Ellen, imploringly; "even at this last moment a reconcilement will be sweet. Think of your early love——"

"With thoughts of the early love, come memories of wrongs and animosities," said Mrs. Hawkshawe, gloomily. "I will not see him. Promise me, all of you, that he shall never know that I did not die years ago, when I left him."

"But he *must* know it soon," urged Mrs. Sweetman. "How can the funeral——"

"He will know nothing of my funeral," interrupted Mrs. Hawkshawe. "There are others besides him to see to that. Life is ebbing fast—will you give me your promise, all of you? I know I can trust you, Reginald, without another pledge."

"I promise," said Ellen, solemnly.

"And so do I," sobbed the housekeeper.

"I am satisfied," said the dying woman; "and now I want another promise from you,

Ellen. You have been Reginald's good angel ever since you came here. You have laboured successfully to undo all the evil that I, his bad angel, have been doing for years. I am going, and your influence will be undivided. This," she said, pointing to the wound in her breast, " this is the last act of the evil spirit. It was my hand, not his, that did it. Do not leave your good work half done. Do not leave him."

" I am bound to remain for a year," faltered Ellen, feeling frightened, as she recalled the bond that held her to that fearful house.

" You will not leave him *then?*" demanded Mrs. Hawkshawe, eagerly. " That is what I mean by leaving your work half done. Think you that all the evil I have implanted in his mind during twenty years can be rooted out by you in twelve months? I own that you have done wonders already, but without you he will relapse; nay, he

will become ten times worse,—he will go
mad. He loves you, Ellen. Promise his
dying mother that you will marry him!"

"Marry him!" cried Ellen, in terror and
astonishment. "Oh no! Never! Never!"

Reginald seized her by the shoulder,
swung her violently round, and held her in
an iron grip, while he glared ferociously
upon her, and said in a voice that resembled
the low growl of a lion, "You will *not*
marry me! Do you hate me, then?"

"I need not hate you, though I cannot
marry you, Reginald," she replied, shrinking under the painful pressure of his muscular hand upon her shoulder. "If there
were no other reason, I could not marry you
while under the dread that at any moment
you may lose your temper, and murder me."

"What is the other reason?" he demanded, sternly.

"You have no right to ask," she said,
trying in vain to release her shoulder.

"She loves some one else, Reginald," said his mother, whose feminine instinct led her at once to the correct interpretation of Ellen's words.

"Is it so, Ellen? Is it so indeed?" said he, mournfully, and dropping his arms.

"I tell you, you have no right to ask me that question," said Ellen; "but as this painful scene must be brought to a close, I will answer you. Yes—I love and am loved; more than that, I am solemnly betrothed!"

"Mother! mother!" cried the young man, throwing himself on his knees, and clasping his mother in his arms, "stay—stay a while—and take me with you!"

"Nay, not so, my son," she replied; "there is long life and happiness in store for you. Hush! be still!" she continued, rising slowly in the bed, while her eyes were fixed upon vacancy, and her forefinger and outstretched right arm pointed as to objects which were passing before her.

"Hush! Speak not! The future is un-rolling to my view—for the last time! Would I might tell all that I see! He shows her the way of escape! Ha! fear not! there is no danger for the firm heart—the steady foot—the resolute will! See how the flames arise! The guilty ones are con-sumed! The boat! the boat!—it will be dashed to pieces! No! It is safe on the sands, and she is rescued. Now is the Death Wail! But not for him! Not for the brave soldier! See! He bears his wounded comrade away amid a shower of rifle balls! That is for her sake—May she one day know it! It is cloudy now—my sight is failing—they pass too quickly, and I cannot see. Ah! one glimpse more! Yes! *They stand at the altar!*"

She fell back into the arms of her son, but so distinct and strong had been her utterance, her action so energetic, that they could not believe that she was dead.

Mrs. Sweetman was the first to discover that life was fled. She communicated the intelligence to Ellen by a look, fearing to rouse the anger of Reginald by telling him what he would so little like to hear.

"Come away," said Ellen, taking him by the arm; "it is useless to remain here. Mrs. Sweetman will see that all proper attention is paid to her remains."

"She is dead, then!" said Reginald, mournfully, as he rose, calm and collected; "the only being who ever loved, or who ever will love me!"

"Do not say that, Reginald," said Ellen, deeply sympathizing with his feeling of desolation—a desolation which she had herself but too keenly experienced. "It depends wholly upon yourself to become tenderly loved by many."

"But not by you, Ellen," he replied; "and I do not care for the love of many. Let us go. You must not stay here, Mrs.

Sweetman," he continued, taking the old lady's hand, and, to her infinite astonishment, pressing it warmly; "I thank you sincerely for your kindness, and your good intentions; but did you not hear *her* say that there were others who would see to her funeral? We must leave her alone, and they will fetch her."

This speech conjured up such awful and supernatural notions that, frightened almost out of her wits, the housekeeper fled from the chamber of death, and sought refuge in Ellen's bedroom, where the cheerful fire imparted an idea of security and companionship.

Reginald returned to the bed, and held the candle so as to throw its light upon the face of the corpse. He stood for some minutes in sorrowful contemplation of the still beautiful features, then pressed a kiss upon the pale cheek, and with a heavy sigh turned away.

"What have I now to live for, Ellen?" he said; "in one night I have lost both mother and hope."

"We can live without hope, Reginald," she replied. "I have lost both my parents, and with them I lost all hope of happiness where I had most expected it. And yet I live on. I do my duty, as far as I am able, and I am cheerful, though not happy."

"Are *you* not happy?" he exclaimed. "Do *you* not hope? Do you mean that you will not be married to—to *him* ?"

"You must not ask me what I mean," said Ellen, in a tone of gentle rebuke. "I could not make you understand it without entering into all the particulars of my life, which it is needless to tell you. What I wished to impress upon you is, that while we do our duty, and submit humbly to the will of Heaven, we cannot be altogether un-happy, though we may be far less happy than we had hoped to be."

"I wish I could know that you were happy, Ellen," said Reginald, looking at her in a thoughtful, dreamy way. "I feel and think a great deal more than I can say, and perhaps I shall not make you understand me; but sometimes I feel that if you tried to go away, or liked any one else better than me, I could kill you. But you know that," he added, with a shuddering glance at the corpse; "you have had a terrible proof how real that dreadful feeling is. It is almost as bad sometimes, when you are playing at chess with my father. I have thought then that I would kill you, and bury you where no one else could find your body, and that I would spend my life at the place where I had put you, and no one should ever look at you again. And then, of late, I have been so delighted to see you look smiling and pleased, even though I have not shared in your pleasure, that I have thought I *must* be happy if you were so. But now, if you do not marry the man you love, you cannot be happy. Why do you not try to love me, Ellen?"

" Love cannot be controlled by the will," she replied. " If it were so, and I could give my affections where my reason tells me I might expect the greatest happiness, I should probably transfer them to you, Reginald—there is so much of native noble-ness and generosity behind your violent and reckless temper. As it is, you must rest contented with my esteem and friend-ship—these you will be sure to have if you continue as you have begun. I shall love you then as much as I should if you were my brother."

" Could you love your brother after *that?*" he asked, pointing to his mother's body, while a shudder passed through his iron frame that told how deeply he felt the con-sequences of his rashness, though he said not much on the subject.

"Yes, and pity him still more," said Ellen, in a tone of deep compassion; "for you would not willingly have hurt her, and your remorse will be lifelong."

"And your own wound," he said, gloomily—"can you pity me after that? Did I not hurt *you* willingly? Did I not try to kill you? Ay—and should have done it had you not started aside at the moment I fired!"

"I pity you for the furious temper which urged you to it, and forgive you the injury you have done me," replied Ellen. "You were mad, and knew not what you did, and for such there was a prayer uttered more than eighteen centuries ago, which ensures pardon."

The young man stood for a moment hesitating whether to speak or not; then in silence led her to the door of her own room.

"Good night, Ellen," he said, kissing her

hand; "do not be frightened if you hear footsteps in this lobby to-night. They will have to come past here," and he glanced towards the room where his mother lay dead.

"I understand you," said Ellen. "But why should she not be honourably buried in the family vault? What is this mysterious funeral that you will give her?"

"It is all done by her own wish," he replied; "do you not know the race to which she belongs?"

"I believe so," said Ellen, with hesitation.

"If you are well enough to-morrow night to bear the fatigue, and the damp air of the dungeons," said Reginald, "you shall witness her funeral. I shall see you before then. Good night."

Ellen re-entered her chamber, and Reginald descended the turret-stairs to the library. With a gloomy brow and a heavy heart he took down the fatal rifle. He gazed on it for some minutes in stern silence, reflecting on the deed that had been done when he last held it in his hands. The cold drops stood upon his brow, and his compressed lip quivered with the sharp agony that wrung his soul.

"Oh, mother! oh, Ellen!" he groaned, rather than uttered. He then charged the gun, but only with powder, and putting two more charges into his pocket, returned to the staircase. Instead of ascending, however, he opened a small arched door, the same that Oliver had pointed out to Ellen as leading to the dungeons.

The door was of immense thickness, very old, and studded with iron. The highly ornamented hinges extended over more than half the width of it, and might have been expected to creak dismally as they moved; but apparently they were kept well oiled, for the heavy door swung back noiselessly, disclosing a flight of stone steps, even more

narrow and steep than those which led to
the upper storey. These Reginald descended with a firm step, which seemed
familiar with their many inequalities.

At some distance below he quitted the
stairs, and passing through another small
door, the key of which was in the lock, he
stood in the open air, near the bottom of
the ravine that was overlooked by the
windows of Ellen's chamber. There was
no moon, but the stars were bright, and gave
sufficient light for one so well acquainted
with his path, dangerous and difficult as
it was. Though near the bottom of the
ravine, he was still some twenty feet above
the level of the brook that roared and rushed
below, when he crossed to the opposite
side by a bridge of very primitive construction, formed by the trunk of a fallen tree. He
walked over with the indifferent air of one
well accustomed to find a safe footing upon
its knotted surface, and began to climb an

intricate and winding path that wound its course up the almost precipitous, though thickly wooded bank.

When he gained the summit he paused and looked at the grim pile of building that crowned the opposite side of the ravine. From two of the windows gleamed a dim lurid light that waxed and waned as the fire-light shone more or less strongly through the closed curtains of Ellen's room. It spoke of life and warmth.

The neighbouring windows were dark, and within them was the icy chill and shadow of death.

A strangely mingled train of thoughts, or rather impulses, of sorrow, remorse, despair, self-destruction, love, hope, determination, and heroic devotion, swept through his brain. He was roused from this kind of reverie by the striking of the old house clock—one, two. He started off over the hills at a rapid pace. Arrived at the top of

a slight eminence at the commencement of
a narrow winding valley between two loftier
hills, he stopped.   There were no visible
signs of any human habitation near; but a
faint smell of burning wood or peat was
plainly perceptible.   He fired his gun; re-
loaded, fired—again a third time, and stood
listening.   In a few seconds three shots
from the neighbouring valley replied; on
hearing which he shouldered his gun and
returned home.

CHAPTER XI.

THE GRAVE BY THE SEA.

THE agitating scenes which Ellen had gone through, and the expectation of hearing the mysterious feet which were to bear their ghastly burden past her door, prevented her from sleeping.

Mrs. Sweetman had taken the precaution of soothing her own nerves with a glass of hot brandy and water, and was soon comfortably asleep; but any such restorative being out of the question in Ellen's case, she lay awake, a prey to the most bewildering phantasies.

She heard the clock strike two, then three;

and still the footsteps of the unknown bear-
ers of the dead had not struck upon her
eagerly listening ears. At length there was
a sound, faint, confused, like the tread of
many muffled feet. She started up, wrapped
a cloak around her, and looked cautiously
out. At the top of the turret-stairs she beheld a group that long remained pictured
in her mind, with its Rembrandt-like effects
of brilliant light and intense shadow.

Two men, of wild and picturesque appearance, bore between them what she knew
must be the body of Mrs. Hawkshawe, enveloped in a large black cloak or pall. They
were just beginning the descent of the stairs.
Reginald stood above, holding a lamp raised
high. The light fell strongly upon his pale
face, contrasting with his bushy beard and
raven hair. A few hours had done upon
his countenance the work of years. He
looked like a man of thirty. The last
Ellen saw of them was when Reginald

stooped to place his hand upon the shoulder of the corpse, lest it should be grazed against the wall. The natural, loving action, brought the tears into her eyes, and when she had dashed them away, the faint reflection from the lamp was alone visible.

On the following afternoon, Reginald begged to be allowed to speak with her. Ellen was struck with his altered manner. Instead of a rough imperious demand, it was a gentle request. She was dressed, and sitting up on the sofa, and admitted him instantly. There was a change in his very walk and carriage. Instead of the wild, bounding step, that had often reminded her of some savage warrior of olden time, his gait was slow, firm, and dignified. His noble head was bowed in thought or grief; but the slight stoop, in place of detracting from his height, served only to make him appear more manly and majestic.

Ellen turned pale as she noticed these

changes, and said to herself, " I *must* go
away."

Had she been questioned as to her reason
for forming this resolve, perhaps she would
have been somewhat puzzled to find it.

Reginald kissed her hand with the gravity
of a Spanish Don, and seated himself on a
chair at a short distance from the sofa.
Here again she saw a difference; formerly
he would have wanted a place by her side,
or on the floor at her feet, with his curly
head lolling on her lap.

" Mrs. Sweetman tells me you are much
better to-day, Ellen," he began.   " I feared
you would be worse after last night," and he
heaved a deep sigh.   " Shall you be strong
enough to bear the fatigue of what I mentioned to you ?"

" Quite strong enough," she replied.

" You will have to go through some very
cold, damp places," said he; " you must
consider it well before you run any risk;

and if you go, you must put on thick boots, and clothe yourself as warmly as possible."

" I have no fear," she replied ; " the fever is quite gone now; I am only rather weak."

" I fear you are *very* weak," he said, with another heavy sigh. "Did you lose much blood ?"

"Not much, I believe," was the reply. " The weakness is in consequence of the fever, together with the low diet, and the effects of fright."

" You lost some blood," he said, taking from his bosom a handkerchief that had been used to bind her arm, and of which he had by some means possessed himself.

" Ah!" cried Ellen, shuddering, " how horrid it looks! Throw it into the fire!"

" Never !" he answered; "at least not yet. If ever you become my wife, Ellen, I will burn this handkerchief, and strive for your sake to think no more of the deed which was done when this blood flowed. Till then its place is here, to remind me of my crimes."

He replaced the handkerchief, and she saw with pain that he put it inside his shirt.

"How can you do so?" she said, with an air of disgust. "How can you be so dirty?"

"Dirty!" he repeated, fixing on her a look in which a wild kind of triumph was the predominant expression. "Ellen, you have never loved!"

"What do you mean?" she asked. "What has that to do with it?"

"Never mind now," he replied. "I hope to teach you the meaning of it one day. Will you remember that I owe you the lesson?"

"You must talk more clearly if you wish me to understand you," she said, coldly.

" When I give you the lesson I will endeavour to be as explicit as possible," said he, rising, and again kissing her hand. He held it for a moment, and then added, with another of his mournful sighs, " I will come for you a little before twelve o'clock, if you are really determined to go."

"It will be a melancholy pleasure, as well as a duty," said Ellen. " I will be ready for you."

He bowed his head, and went out of the room.

" Dear me !" half-soliloquised Mrs. Sweetman. "Only to think that the other day, as might be, he could scarcely speak at all; and now he talks dictionary words as clever as anybody."

Ellen could almost have smiled at the old lady's quaint remark, but other and more serious thoughts then occupied her mind. She took a prayer-book from the table by her side, and opening it at the service for the dead, remained for the whole evening earnestly studying it, and committing to memory the greater part of the prayers. The housekeeper saw how she was occupied, guessed at the object she had in view, and held a respectful silence.

At half-past eleven Reginald knocked softly at the door, and found Ellen prepared to accompany him. He would not rest satisfied until he had examined her boots, and convinced himself that they were thick enough to protect her from the ill effects of the cold damp floorings of the dungeons. Her cloak then underwent a scrutiny, after which he led her away, recommending Mrs. Sweetman to lie down and sleep till their return.

Ellen shivered as the chill air blew on her when the little door was opened. Her companion perceived it, and wrapped round her a large fur railway rug, which hung by the library door.

"It is too heavy," said Ellen, trying to disengage herself from its voluminous folds. "I could not walk in it."

"I don't expect you to do so," he replied; and taking her in his arms, he carried her down the steep and broken stairs as easily as if she had been an infant.

Ellen was not a sylph. She had a tall, well-developed figure, and she possessed more strength and activity than usually belong to girls in these degenerate days. In the times that Spenser sings of, she might have been a Britomart, or coming nearer to actualities, a Joan of Arc. She knew, too, that Reginald was strong—very strong; but she had formed no accurate notion of *how* strong, until now, when she found herself as helpless as a child in those Titanic arms.

"He can never be my pupil again," she thought; "I can never recover even the semblance of authority. I can walk now—

I would rather walk," she said aloud, and trying to struggle.

"Little fool! keep quiet, or you will knock your head against the wall," was his half-angry reply.

"But I prefer walking," said Ellen.

"And I prefer carrying you," he replied.

"You hurt my arm," she said. This was true, but it was her own fault for moving it.

Instantly he stopped, re-adjusted the wrapper, took her up again, and went on. They were in total darkness, but he walked with the unhesitating step of a blind man who knows his way. Presently a gleam of light shot across the narrow staircase. They passed through another door which stood open, and there Reginald set Ellen down, seated her on a chair that was placed ready for her, covered her carefully with the rug, and whispering, "Stay here till I come for you," quitted her and walked

towards the spot whence the light proceeded.

Ellen had now time to look about her.
The place in which she found herself was
a long narrow chamber, with a high vaulted
roof, and no apparent communication with
the outer air. The floor was paved, and at
intervals along the walls were stone seats,
rudely shaped. In the wall above the one
nearest to her she noticed an iron ring from
which depended a rusty chain. No doubt
the rest were similarly furnished; more
than suggesting the idea that this horrible
place had echoed to the groans of miserable
captives, the victims of feudal or priestly
tyranny.

Little leisure, however, had she for these
observations, ere her attention was riveted
upon a group of persons who were assembled
about midway down the vault. There were
thirteen of them, among whom the com-
manding figure of Reginald towered pre-

eminent. In the centre of this group was
a stone bench, resembling those along the
walls, and on this lay the body of Mrs.
Hawkshawe, covered with a pall. Six of
the men who stood round, bore lighted
torches that cast a bright though fitful
light upon the scene, the low-arched ceiling,
the massive walls, and the silent and motionless figures, all clad alike in long
mourning cloaks.

Ellen gazed in wondering expectation of
what would be done next, as they were
evidently waiting for something. Presently
the tread of many feet was heard, proceed-
ing from the lower end of the dungeon, and
a crowd of wild-looking men and women,
dimly visible by the light of a few scattered
torches, came hurriedly on. They crowded
round the rude bier, each eager to get a look
at the face of the corpse, and then, following
an old crone, bent nearly double by age,
who raised her shrill pipe to give the key,

they commenced a low wailing dirge. Ellen
had listened to the finest compositions of
the greatest musicians, with full orchestra
and a noble organ, but nothing so thrilling,
so terrible in its wild pathos, as that gipsy
dirge, had she ever heard. The women's
voices sometimes rose into almost a shriek
of agony, then sank into a low dismal wail;
the voices of the men were never loud, but
the great volume of sound from so many
strong bass throats, singing in unison, had
an effect beyond that of the mightiest organ.
Perhaps the strange wildness of the scene,
and her own weakened nerves, had something to do with it—but her senses reeled,
and seemed about to forsake her.

In the midst of the chant, the six men
who did not carry torches lifted the litter
on which the corpse lay, and bore it away
down the vault, followed by the crowd,
huddled promiscuously together. Reginald
returned to Ellen, drew the hood of her

16—2

cloak down so as to conceal her features, and taking her by the hand, led her after the strange funeral procession. They left the vault by another door, resembling that by which they had entered it, and Ellen, after some clambering among broken fragments of rock, was surprised to find herself on the beach of the small bay, so enclosed by precipitous rocks that there seemed to be no access to it except by boats. The brook that rushed through the glen below her window, and whose wild music had so often lulled her to sleep, here formed an estuary; and a cascade, which she rightly judged proceeded from a stream in the garden, sprang down the rugged face of the rocks in a halo of spray and foam. The moon was at the full, and gave to view the whole scene in hasty snatches, as the dense black clouds that scudded tumultuously across the sky, left for a moment a clear space around her. Ellen was scarcely conscious

at the time of observing all this, or thinking about it at all, but it made an impression on her mind that lasted long after.

The clouds gathered thicker, and the
dim light of the torches alone cast a lurid
glare upon the wild figures that stood
round an open grave, dug in the sands
above high-water mark. The wind moaned
and whistled as wild and shrill as the
voices of the women, and the sullen boom-
ing of the sea lent a yet deeper bass to the
funeral chorus. Ellen clung to Reginald's
arm, and for a moment the deathly faintness
again came over her. She thought it must
be all some terrible dream—that it could not
be a reality. But she quickly recovered
herself. The consciousness of having her
prayer-book in her hand recalled her by
reminding her of the purpose for which she
had brought it. But there was not light
enough to read by, and therefore she began,
in a low but clear voice, to repeat those

parts of the burial service which she had learned. The young man bowed his head and listened. She caught his reverent, attentive look, and spoke with increased distinctness; and had the satisfaction of hearing him join in the deep *Amen*.

With no ceremonial but that lugubrious chant, which was more like a charm to scare away evil spirits, than a prayer for mercy and redemption, the funeral ended. The sand was shovelled in upon the un-coffined body, and all made smooth and level above, leaving no mound to mark the grave. All stood silent for a moment; then one man fetched a large stone and placed it over her; all followed his example, and a cairn of considerable size was piled up in a few minutes. All now looked at Reginald. With but little effort he took up an enor-mous boulder, which two of the men had vainly endeavoured to stir, and placed it gently on the summit of the cairn. Then

he waved his arm to them as if in dismissal.
They bowed before him, and hastened without speaking to two large boats that were
drawn up on the beach. Reginald stood
silent till they had all embarked, and put
off upon the troubled sea.

"I have killed their queen," he said, in a
solemn tone; "and yet *they* do not account
me a murderer. How am I accounted
there?" and he pointed upwards.

"Not as a murderer, Reginald," said
Ellen. "Not even human justice could
accuse you of being the wilful cause of her
death."

"My keenest accuser is here, Ellen," said
he, pointing to his breast. "Do not
suppose that the voice is still, if I never
again speak on this subject. She rests
there in her lonely grave; but her memory
will live in her son's heart, wild and wicked
as it is. Come—you are not strong enough
to bear all this fatigue."

Ellen added a stone to the cairn, and they re-entered the dungeon.

A torch had been stuck into one of the iron rings, to give them light across the vault. Reginald left it to burn itself out, as there was nothing to catch fire in the place, and wrapped his companion tenderly round in the fur rug, preparatory to carrying her up the stairs.

"No, no," she said, trying to resist, "I will not be carried, Reginald! I will walk."

"The stairs are so broken and steep that you would fall at every step," he replied, coolly taking her up; "and there is not room for me to keep beside you. You must submit to necessity, though perhaps it prevents your feeling very much like my *governess*."

"I already feel that that position is given up from necessity," said Ellen, stung by the tone of irony in which he uttered the last word; " and very soon it must be entirely abandoned."

There was a furious involuntary contraction of the muscles of his arms, and a grinding of his set teeth, but it was only momentary. He subdued the passion, and said calmly, " We will talk about that to-morrow."

At the door of her room he set her down, thanked her, blessed her in a hurried choking voice, kissed both her hands with tender affection, and stalked away down the long passage.

Ellen was glad to seek the repose of her own bed; and notwithstanding the strange scenes through which she had just passed, she was so wearied that she sank at once into a deep slumber. Mrs. Sweetman was sound asleep on the sofa, and an empty tumbler on the table showed that she had taken the precaution of "soothing her nerves" before composing herself to rest.

CHAPTER XII.

LOVE AND LEARNING.

THE following morning Mr. Hawkshawe
was somewhat surprised at receiving a mes-
sage from his son, requesting his presence
in the library.

They had not met since the fatal day of
the accident; and so painfully vivid was
that scene before his mental vision, and so
little did he relish the idea of being exposed
in a *tête-à-tête* to the young man's ungovernable temper, that he took the precaution of
putting a loaded pistol into his pocket,
before complying with the summons.

On entering the library, the first glance
entirely dispelled all his apprehensions.

With his arms folded thoughtfully across his breast, Reginald was slowly pacing up and down the room. Hector lay upon the hearth-rug; but sympathizing with his master's altered mood, did not even utter a growl at the approach of his old enemy.

Mr. Hawkshawe's surprise was increased when Reginald deferentially placed a chair for him, and, opening the window, dismissed the dog into the garden.

"I wish to consult you, sir, about my studies," Reginald began, without a moment's hesitation, as he turned from the window. "It is ridiculous for me any longer to learn of a girl, clever as she is, and much as I love her."

"I am delighted to hear you speak so rationally," replied his father; "but for the present," he added, with considerable hesitation of manner, "it is very much against my wish that Miss Maynard should quit my house."

"May I ask your reasons, sir?" said Reginald, sitting down opposite to his father, and looking steadfastly, almost sternly, in his face.

"My reasons—my reasons are immaterial in the question now pending," stammered Mr. Hawkshawe; "at least, they do not concern you, and I imagine I am not accountable for either my motives or my actions, to my own son."

"Certainly not, sir," replied Reginald, coolly, "excepting in as far as they affect Miss Maynard, in whom I have, of course, a stronger interest than you can possibly feel."

Mr. Hawkshawe compressed his lips, and his cheeks turned white with anger. What made matters worse, was that he knew his son was watching him with those calm black eyes, in all the dignity of his newly-acquired self-control.

At length throwing off his temporary

embarrassment, he said, "Let us continue the subject on which you desired to consult me, Reginald. Do you wish to go to college?"

"No, sir; decidedly no," said the young man, firmly. "Miss Maynard has taught me enough to enable me to see how little I know. I should cut a silly figure, I am aware, among any set of young men of even tolerable education, and I fear my temper would not stand the ridicule I should meet with. Besides which, I know I can make greater progress under another system. I wish Dr. Gibson to come for several hours every day, as he did before, but for a longer time. I will continue to learn music of Ellen—Miss Maynard, I mean—and to read with her."

"I think your plan a very good one," said the elder gentleman; "that is, if you can adhere to it."

"Do not fear that, sir," said Reginald.

" As it meets your approval I should like to put it in action without delay. Will you go to Dr. Gibson this morning, or shall I ?"

" *This morning!*" repeated Mr. Hawkshawe. " You have formed your resolution very quickly, and you seem determined to commence carrying it out with the same haste."

" I feel that I have no time to lose, sir," said his son; "besides, promptitude and decision belong to our family, I believe."

" I will go then, at once, to Dr. Gibson," said his father; "but *his* wishes have to be consulted, as well as ours."

" He'll come," said Reginald, confidently. " Tell him he will have nothing now to fear from my hasty temper."

" Upon whose assurance can I tell him that?" asked his father, with a slight sneer.

" I think, sir, you may speak from experience," replied the young man, with perfect equanimity; and his father felt that he

might; for three days before he would not
have ventured to say one of the annoying
and sarcastic things that Reginald had to-
day taken so calmly.

" Well then, I will go to him," said Mr.
Hawkshawe, rising, " and ask him to come,
I suppose, to-morrow morning."

".This afternoon if he can," said Reginald;
" he cannot come too soon."

" I will tell him your wish," said his
father. " By the bye," he added, turning
at the door, which, to his utter amazement,
Reginald had respectfully opened, " have
you heard how Miss Maynard is this morning?"

"She is much better, sir, thank you,"
replied Reginald.

Acknowledging the answer by a slight
inclination of the head, Mr. Hawkshawe
passed out.

" Impertinent puppy !" he muttered,
as he strode impatiently across the hall ;

"why should he thank me for inquiring after Ellen's health? And by what right has he a stronger interest in her than I have? I must get him off to college. And yet, in that case, what excuse should I have for detaining her? No—there can be no danger in letting them be together. She must dislike and fear him for the violence that put her life in peril. Yet what a change has come over him! I cannot understand him, nor myself. I have attained what was my most ardent wish, and yet I am not satisfied!"

As soon as Reginald was alone, he sat down to the piano, and practised diligently for an hour or two. So absorbed was he in his exercises that he did not observe Ellen enter the room. Rising at length to admit Hector, whose impatient whining had attracted his notice, he saw his fair monitress sitting in an easy-chair, reading.

"Ellen!" he exclaimed, kneeling on one

knee at her feet, and possessing himself of her hand, which he covered with kisses, "how long have you been here?"

"About half an hour," she replied, "and I was glad to hear you practising so diligently. If you go on so you will soon play well."

"I mean to work hard at everything," he said, "I have had a consultation with my father this morning, and he has gone to ask Dr. Gibson to come again as he used to do."

"Do you think Dr. Gibson will venture to become your instructor again, Reginald?" asked Ellen. "From what you have told me of your conduct towards him, and what I have heard from others, I should imagine he would be too fearful of your violent temper, to come willingly within range of it."

"Oh! Ellen! Ellen!" he said, bowing his face upon her knee, "can I ever again give

way to a fit of rage? This dear wounded
arm, and that other—which I dare not
speak of—are these not sufficient to make
me control my temper?"

" Sufficient to make you strive earnestly
to do so, at least," said Ellen ; " but *really*
to control it, after long indulgence, is one
of the most difficult things to accomplish."

"I have gone through one trial already,
with my father," said Reginald, " and I
found it easy enough. It was amusing,
though ; he looked so astonished."

"No doubt he did," said Ellen; "now
let Hector in, or he will break the
window."

" There is one thing, Ellen, that I will
not stand upon any terms," said Reginald,
impatiently.

" What is that ?" she asked.

" You must not treat me as a child in one
respect, and not in another, just as it suits
your own purpose," he replied.

"I don't understand you," said Ellen. "I cannot treat you as a child."

"You *do*," he said, "so it seems that you can. You tell me to let the dog in, as if I were a child, and could not discover that your real reason is that you do not like a man to press this little smooth soft hand between his own great rough ones, thus; nor lay his bearded face upon your lap, in this fashion. Now, Ellen, before I let go this hand, or raise my head, tell me how old you are? You are no longer my governess, you know, and I am no longer a boy."

"I am perfectly aware of both those facts," she replied; "I am twenty years old."

"And I," said he, "I am two-and-twenty! Perhaps I ought to be ashamed of this, as I am so ignorant. But I am not, Ellen. I am pleased at being older than you, and the ignorance shall quickly be got rid of."

"I shall always be glad to hear of your progress," said Ellen. "I have no doubt Dr. Gibson, or his sister, will write frequently to me."

"So you think you are going to make your escape, my lady fair?" said Reginald, with a faint smile. "No, no, Ellen, you must not go," he added, gravely; "without you I can do nothing. *You must not leave your work half finished.*"

As he said this, he rose and let in the dog.

"We *must* come to an understanding," said Ellen, after a pause. "You must be made to comprehend how much I shall suffer in the estimation of the world—of every one who hears of it—by living here any longer. I appeal to your generosity, Reginald—to your justice."

"If it depended only upon me, Ellen, I could not refuse you," said the young man. "I would rather know that you were happy

though away from me, than keep you here
to fret in what you feel to be a sort of cap-
tivity. But it does not depend upon me.
My father will not let you go."

Ellen's eyes filled with tears at his generous disinterestedness.

" There—there—comfort yourself !" he
continued, wiping away her tears. " I will
try to persuade my father to release you
from your engagement. You shall never
be unhappy, dear Ellen, while I can do anything to cheer you, even though your happiness depends upon your being relieved
from my presence."

" You mistake me, Reginald," she said ;
" it is not that ; it is from a feeling of propriety——"

" Well, well," he said, interrupting her,
" never mind the explanation. You wish
it—that is enough ; and if possible I will
get it done ; but I cannot give you much
hope, for my father spoke very positively

about it this morning. Now let me read to you till dinner-time."

" Poor Reginald !" thought Ellen—"dear Reginald! He speaks of *my* hopes, not of his own! Am I too selfish in desiring to leave him?—oh, Frank, it is for your sake !"

" Have you any objection to my reading the newspaper to you, Ellen?" asked Reginald, unfolding the *Times.* " I know so little of what goes on in the world, that if I went among strangers I should seem as though I had dropped down from the moon. I may learn from Dr. Gibson and from books all that happened long ago, but I fancy it must be quite as important to know what is happening at the present time."

" Certainly it is," she replied; "and I shall be very glad to hear you; for I have scarcely seen a paper since I came here, and therefore I know as little as yourself of what is passing in the world."

Reginald read the leading articles one by

one, with many pauses for explanation, where his acquaintance with dates, persons, events and geography, was not sufficient to enable him fully to understand the meaning of what he read. It was shortly before the declaration of war with Russia, and the imminence of that event was treated of with the utmost confidence. Ellen's heart beat fast with many anxious feelings as he went on.

"*If* there is war," was her natural reflection, "what regiments will be sent out? Will Frank go?"

Reginald also felt deeply interested, for he exclaimed, "I wish I were a soldier!—but even soldiers, at least officers, must know a great deal more than I do! Oh, Ellen, how I regret having thrown away the opportunity of learning, when first I came to this house! If I had studied then, I might now have been able to be a soldier. It is worth while to be one, now that there

is real fighting! Ah! here they tell us
what regiments are ordered to be placed on
a war footing. Happy fellows! I wish I
were one of you!"

He read on. But at the mention of one
regiment Ellen, being still weak and nervous
from her wound, screamed and fainted.
Mrs. Sweetman was speedily in attendance,
and the young lady was restored. Reginald
said nothing about the cause of her illness,
not even to herself, but he made a note of
the regiment the name of which had so
affected her.

In the afternoon Dr. Gibson arrived.

Ellen felt slightly indisposed, but she ex-
erted herself to give a cordial welcome to
the good old man, whose society she had
always wished to cultivate from the first
time she heard him preach, but from which
she had been debarred by Reginald's furious
conduct towards him, which had prevented
his coming near the house until the present

time. Ellen was aware that although a sense of duty might oblige him to undertake the education of the young savage when called upon to do so, yet he must feel somewhat uneasy on first entering the lion's den; and she wished by her own manner to reassure him.

The matter was settled at once, however, and in a much easier way, by Reginald himself. Stepping up to the doctor, he held out his hand, and frankly and modestly asked his pardon for his former rudeness; then looked at Ellen for the approving smile with which he knew she would reward him. The smile was ready for him, and much warmer and kinder than she would have suffered it to be, had she been less taken by surprise. The old clergyman was quite overpowered; but that quickly passed, and his impatient pupil commenced his studies.

It is needless to follow Reginald in his labours further than to say that he worked with so much industry and will, that he accomplished in a day more than many learn in a week or a month. Besides the hours he spent with his tutor, he practised the piano assiduously, and studied by himself till after midnight, rising again after three or four hours' sleep, to resume his preparations for the day's work. In addition to all this he never once omitted reading the *Times* aloud to Ellen. Still, not a word did he utter about her fainting at the name of a certain regiment, nor was that regiment mentioned again in the papers for some weeks.

Ellen showed a feverish interest in all that concerned the war and the movements of the army, and Reginald was equally anxious to read every word to her. His indignation knew no bounds against those degenerate sons—surely not of England, but of some chance denizens of the land— who sold their commissions rather than face the enemy.

Ellen joined in his feelings, but timidly and nervously, not that she feared that Frank Willoughby would be a craven, but "he was the only son of his mother, and she was a widow," and she feared lest his mother should so value his life above his honour, as to induce him to yield to her tears and entreaties. Reginald observed that she checked and qualified her condemnation of these unhappy creatures, and he controlled the ebullition of his own wrath, divining why she did so, and careful not to pain her. But he thought in his own proud heart, "If *I* were her lover, she would have no fear of hitting me a chance blow, while heaping contempt on these poltroons! I would not change places with him, even to have her love; for she mistrusts him. She could feel for me a higher love than that, if she once began to love me!"

Then she made excuses for them, and said perhaps they were good sons, and their mothers would break their hearts if they

went into battle; perhaps there were some
of them only sons of widows; and he drew
the inference that all this was said for the
sake of one who *was* a widow's only son.
And Reginald felt pleased at his discovery,
though he still kept it to himself.

Meantime his brown cheek became hollow
and sallow through want of sleep and out-
door exercise, and from the closeness of his
studies.

"Never mind!" he said, when Ellen remonstrated with him, "I am strong enough
to bear much more than this. A few days
among the hills will make all right again;
and I *must* get on fast, for I have an object
to gain."

What that object was, Reginald would not
confess, though he always pleaded it as a
reason for sacrificing every other consideration to the vigorous prosecution of his
studies. Dr. Gibson was amazed at his
progress. Mr. Hawkshawe was delighted,

yet inclined to give all the credit to Ellen, who had first given the impetus to her pupil's vigorous intellect. She was delighted too, and not averse to receive her share of the praise, for she knew how hard she had toiled to awaken in him a desire for knowledge for its own sake.

Reginald alone seemed to feel no pleasure in his own progress, except sometimes when Ellen praised him. He worked on with steady determination, yet with no apparent enjoyment, and she knew that unless when his mind was thus occupied he was for ever brooding on the death of his mother, and his own share in it. She even doubted whether the idea was not always present to his mind, though in a latent condition; hardly as a thought, but as a dim feeling, like pain that is felt in sleep.

In the concentration of deep study, and probably hereafter in the occupations of active life, lay the surest remedy for this

gnawing sorrow, which he must always feel
with more or less acuteness; and she wisely
encouraged him in his labours, and resolved
to say nothing about her departure till the
term of her agreement had expired.

CHAPTER XIII.

HOW ELLEN'S LETTERS WENT ASTRAY.

ANXIETIES of her own now began to press heavily upon Ellen.

There had been no special mention of Frank Willoughby's name from the seat of war, nor had the name of every renegade officer been gibbeted for public execration.

Meantime the Crimean war had commenced in good earnest, and the first news of him might be in the list of slain; or from some private source she might learn that he had become unworthy of the love of any true-born English girl.

If this were the case, Ellen would probably find apologies for him in his mother's weak and anxious love; she would pity him; she would not confess to despising him; but she would not marry him.

In the midst of her anxious ruminations she suddenly recollected her determination, made on the night after she was wounded, to write again to Mr. Smedley, and to drop the letter in the village on her way from church, which was the only occasion on which she could ever get so far towards the post-office. This plan she carried into execution on the following Sunday, and an epistle, containing the fullest local information that she could give, was written to the good doctor. This she placed behind a tombstone as she passed, under the watchful escort of Mr. Hawkshawe, from the church door to the carriage.

In the afternoon, while she was indulging in fond dreams of what *might* happen in consequence of the safe arrival of that letter at its destination, the library door was burst open, and Reginald entered hastily. His face was flushed, and his eyes glowing with suppressed anger. He shut the door more gently than he had opened it, but it required an effort to keep him from slamming it. He leaned upon the mantel-piece, grinding his heel into the rug, and gnawing his "nether lip," while he looked at Ellen, but did not trust himself to speak.

Ellen saw that he was struggling for mastery over the passion that possessed him like a demon; and going quietly to the piano, she played some music of a soothing and tender character, adding as much as possible to its plaintiveness by the manner of performing. Reginald came to her side after a while, but she went on without noticing him. At length his murmured thanks fell upon her ear, and then she knew that he had overcome his hitherto invincible enemy, and could trust himself to speak. She was anxious to know what

had moved him so deeply, yet would not
risk awakening the demon again by asking
any questions. She paused, but only as if
to look out another piece of music.

"Why don't you ask what has made me
so angry?" said Reginald.

"Because if it is anything that you wish
me to know, you will tell me without being
asked," she replied, turning from the
piano.

"I thought women were always inquisitive," said Reginald.

"Not all women, I hope," said Ellen;
"but without being inquisitive, I may feel
a lively interest in whatever affects my
friends. I am *very* anxious to know what
has vexed you, but I have no right to pry
into what does not concern me."

"It does concern you," he replied, his
brow growing black again. "You dropped
a letter in the churchyard this morning.
Was that done on purpose?"

"Did your father see it?" cried Ellen, in alarm.

"In heaven's name! why should he *not* see it?" exclaimed Reginald, impetuously. "Why should you use any subterfuge to get your letters posted? Would they not go safely in the bag with the rest?"

"Do not accuse me of entertaining unfounded suspicions till you know all the facts of the case," said Ellen. "I have written twice to a friend since I came here, and have had no answer to either of my letters. Without being very suspicious, what can I imagine but that my letters have been intercepted, especially when I recollect that your father, in our first interview, appeared excessively anxious about my correspondents?"

"I don't accuse you of being suspicious, my dear girl," said Reginald; "the only fault I find with you is that you did not trust your letters to me to be posted. If

18—2

you will write another I'll undertake that
it shall be delivered by hand, and an answer
brought back, as fast as the mail train can
go, and horses' feet scamper."

"You have not told me what has become
of the other," said Ellen. "Did your father
see me drop it?"

"No," replied Reginald; "I'll tell you all
about it. I went to Mr. Hawkshawe's
room just now to give him a list of the books
that I want from London; and while I was
there, the postmaster came in with a letter,
which he said had been picked up in the
churchyard by the sexton, and which he
thought was in the hand-writing that '*his
honour*' had ordered him to bring to him,
and it was also directed the same as the
others, to Mr. Smedley. All this he blurted
out without seeing me, and before *his honour*
could stop his tongue, I saw that the address
on the letter was in your hand, and I tried
to get possession of it, but my—No!—I'll

never call him father again!—he—Mr.
Hawkshawe threw it into the fire. I tell
you, Ellen, that even the terrible consequences of my last explosion of rage could
scarcely enable me to command myself. I
would not trust myself to speak or look at
him, so I came away. And now do you
wonder that I was angry?"

"My greatest wonder is that being so
angry, you had power to control your
anger," said Ellen.

"I *must* do that, Ellen," he said, with a
sigh so deep that it was almost a groan.
"Think what I have already done in a fit
of rage! That thought is always with me,
and I will bite out my tongue, and strike off
my right hand before I burden my memory
with another such reflection."

"You have already done yourself some
mischief!" she cried, as a drop of blood
trickled from his beard. "Oh! Reginald!
what *have* you done?"

"It is only my lip," he replied, quietly. "I bit it to help in keeping down my anger."

"You have bitten it almost through!" she said, wiping the blood away with her handkerchief, while her eyes filled with tears.

Reginald smiled with delight when he saw her tears. The smile opened the wound afresh, and it bled fast.

"Why do you smile?" said she. "Keep your mouth quiet, or the bleeding will not stop."

"I am smiling at your tears," he answered, fondly, "and I would kiss them off your cheeks, but that in doing so I should smear them with this nasty dirty red stuff. Here—give me that handkerchief,—let me throw it into the fire".

"No—no," cried she, holding it back, when he tried to snatch it, "a few drops of blood are easily washed off. Besides, I want the clean part to wipe my eyes."

He threw himself into an easy chair, crossed his legs, and gazed thoughtfully into the fire for some minutes, mechanically compressing his lacerated lip with his own handkerchief in the meanwhile. And Ellen felt that in some unaccountable way their relative positions had undergone a further change. How was it, she thought, that every incident, great or small, seemed to give him an increased ascendancy over her? While she was trying to solve this enigma, Reginald's voice interrupted her, speaking in low, sad tones.

"Write another letter, Ellen," he said, "and it shall go safely. You will write freely, and as your heart dictates, will you not; and feel quite sure that it will go securely through my hands, and be as sacred as my own honour?"

"Indeed, I shall, Reginald," she replied, looking trustingly into his eyes. "Why do you for a moment imagine that I should doubt you?"

" You have every right to doubt me," he
said, bitterly. "Like father, like son, they
say. Were the other letters you mentioned
addressed to the same person?"

" Yes," replied Ellen.

"And those he may have opened and
read!" exclaimed Reginald, writhing as if
in bodily pain. "All the unrestrained expressions of your fond heart (for I know
you *can* be fond, Ellen!)—all the tender
words meant for but one eye in all this
world, *he* may have gloated over!"

This speech enlightened her upon two
points—first, that Reginald believed that
her letters had been written to her lover;
and secondly, that he thought his father
was in love with her. Some unpleasant
surmises on this latter question had for
some time past forced themselves upon her
own mind.

"And he would send my letters to a
supposed rival!" she mentally exclaimed.

" He is indeed generous!—Magnanimous!
I must undeceive him—but how shall I do
it?"

" Smedley!" said Reginald, musingly,
after a pause of some five minutes' duration,
" Smedley! It is not a very good name,
is it, Ellen—not so good as the one you
already bear?"

" It belongs to a very good man, though,"
said she; " he is one of the pleasantest,
kindest old gentlemen I ever met with."

" Old!" exclaimed Reginald, starting up.
" You are not going to marry an old man?"

" I am not going to marry any one yet,"
she replied, laughing: " and least of all,
Mr. Smedley."

" What a fool I am!" cried Reginald,
laughing also, as he subsided into his chair
again. " I could not imagine you writing
to any one but your lover. Who, then, is
this Mr. Smedley, if I may ask?"

" He is the doctor who attended my

father during his last illness," replied Ellen, relapsing into the gravity that was usual with her, " and he is besides the only friend who remained unchanged when it was known that I was left poor instead of rich."

" The *only* friend?" repeated Reginald, inquiringly. " I wish you would tell me frankly all about it. I don't ask from mere curiosity. Was there not *one* other friend who would not desert you?"

" I understand whom you mean," said Ellen, hesitating and blushing; " he was abroad, and knew nothing about it."

" And his friends—his family—were they abroad too?" he continued.

" He has only his mother," she replied; " no other near relatives."

" Did she turn the cold shoulder on you in your adversity?" he inquired.

" Do not press these questions on me, Reginald!" cried Ellen, bursting into tears.

" I'll ask you no more, my dear girl—I

know enough now," said Reginald; and he began to walk thoughtfully up and down the room—a habit which he had acquired since he became studious.

After a few turns the young man stopped, raised Ellen's face by putting his hand under her chin, looked at her steadily for a minute or two, then gravely kissed her on the forehead, and bade her write her letter quickly, for he wanted her to play to him.

" By the by," said Reginald, as Ellen was folding the letter, "you had better tell him to enclose his answer under cover to Dr. Gibson. Mr. Hawkshawe might think proper to detain it."

" Dr. Gibson would think it strange, not knowing all the circumstances," said Ellen.

"Then bid him enclose it in another envelope directed to John Lynch, blacksmith, St. Mawes," said Reginald, "and add, that you have reason to suspect that your letters have been tampered with in the post-office here, that is—unless you have already told him——"

"I have told him nothing that might bring disgrace upon a name which *you*, I am sure, will make honourably known," replied Ellen.

"Thank you, dearest, thank you for those kind words," said Reginald.

"Mr. Smedley will wonder at my taking a blacksmith into my confidence," said Ellen; "how shall I account for that?"

"Just leave him to think what he likes," replied Reginald; "he will probably imagine that he is a friend of one of the servants. You may be sure he will suppose nothing wrong of you."

"But who is John Lynch?" she asked, as she sealed the letter.

"A friend of mine," said Reginald; "indeed, a distant relation."

Ellen stared at him with astonishment. He replied by a look into which he threw

so much of the gipsy character that she
blushed at her own obtuseness. He smiled
as he took the letter from her, and then
handed her to the piano.

Mr. Hawkshawe did not make his appearance that evening, and for several days
Ellen saw nothing of him. She had determined to avoid letting him know that
Reginald had acquainted her with his dis-
honourable conduct respecting her letters,
and had even persuaded the young man
himself to forbear any allusion to the subject when he saw his father. Consequently
when, towards the end of the week, she
accidentally encountered Mr. Hawkshawe,
there was nothing in her manner to lead
him to suppose she was aware that he
had tampered with her correspondence.
" Humph," he soliloquised, " I am glad to
see that Reginald has so much family
pride."

By return of post Ellen received, under

cover to John Lynch, a long letter from
Mr. Smedley, expressing the liveliest satisfaction at hearing of her well-being, and
letting her off, for that once only, as he
emphatically declared, without the sharp
lecture he had mentally prepared for her
any day these six months, upon the sin of
dilatoriness in writing letters to old friends.

"The fact is, my dear young lady," he
concluded, " I have been exceedingly uneasy
about you, especially since I learned from
Mrs. Mason (to whom—shall I confess it?—I
made a purpose journey) the extraordinary
manner in which you had been carried
off. I am indeed thankful to hear of your
safety. * * *

"You ask news of myself. What news
could there be worth telling of a frowsy
old bachelor, always busy tinkering up his
fellow-mortals? I am not married; that
is all I can say about myself, but many
of your acquaintances are." Here he gave

a page or two to the gossip of the neigh-
bourhood. "I am rather busy just now,"
he continued, in a postscript written across
one corner, "which must be my excuse for
sending you such a disconnected letter.
The public health is good, but my best
patient, Lady Willoughby, is suffering from
nerves, in consequence of her son's determination to stick to his colours and his
regiment, and go out with them to Turkey,
instead of coming home at his mammy's
bidding, like a good boy; or rather, as I
often long to tell her ladyship, like a whipped
cur with his tail between his legs. I try
my best to convince her that he has taken
the only right and honourable course; and
when I find it all in vain, I pocket my fee,
and send her a soothing draught. Captain
W. writes in high spirits. He reports himself in prime health, and delighted with
camp life. All which ought to satisfy any
mother, unless she were a fool."

"She has news of him," thought Reginald, who had watched Ellen, over his book, while she read this letter. "He remains with his regiment! I see it in her pale cheek, in her full bright eye, in the proud curl of her lip, in her arching neck, in her expanded chest, in the deep sigh that struggles painfully from it. Yes—he remains with his regiment. Good—now I must discover his name."

CHAPTER XIV.

REGINALD LOSES FAITH IN HIS TUTOR.—
A VISIT TO THE HERMITAGE.

DURING some months Reginald's energies never relaxed for a single hour, with the exception of the very few which he allotted to sleep. Incessant study—unwearied labour.

Change of occupation was the only respite he allowed· himself. When not engaged with Dr. Gibson, he was studying music and modern languages with Ellen; and for hours after she was gone to bed, and before she appeared at breakfast, as well as at every spare minute before and after meals, he was pursuing a course of reading on a plan of his own.

One afternoon Reginald was so absorbed in the perusal of a book, that he did not observe the entrance of his tutor. The old gentleman looked over his shoulder, and started back aghast.

"My dear young friend!" he exclaimed, "what book are you reading?"

"Carlyle's 'Hero-Worship,'" replied Reginald, looking up with a face glowing with animation and delight—"is it not a glorious work?"

"I am grieved," said the good old clergyman, shaking his head, "deeply grieved to see that your young mind is captivated and entangled in that network of false philosophy and immorality."

"*Immorality!*" repeated Reginald. "I think, sir, you have mistaken the book. I am near the end, and not one sentence have I read that is not full of the highest, and deepest, and widest morality."

"When I speak of its immoral tendency,"

said Dr. Gibson, "I mean that it is irreligious."

"There again you are wrong, sir," persisted Reginald, firmly but respectfully; "for I never felt a religious sentiment till I read this work. I should say the writer was a most religious man."

"He may be—he may be in one sense," said Dr. Gibson; "that is, he may perhaps have a vague, undefined sort of religious feeling, what is called natural religion; but he scoffs at revealed religion."

"Pardon me, sir," said Reginald—"in *this* book, at least, he scoffs at no religion, but holds all creeds that are truly believed in to be worthy of respect even by those who have no faith in them."

"That is the very point I am trying to impress upon you," said the old gentleman, with vivacity. "A man who professes to reverence every creed under the sun, can have no fixed faith of his own. Why, the

19—2

very name of that book is enough. ' Hero-
Worship!' What can be the religion of
that man who would worship mere heroes?
Worship is due to *One* alone!"

" I understood you to say *three* the other
day, sir," observed Reginald, with quiet
malice; but seeing Ellen shake her head
reprovingly, he added, before the old gentleman had time to snatch up his weapons in
defence of the Trinity, " have you read this
book, sir?"

" God forbid that a man of my cloth
should find no better use for his time on
earth than in reading atheistical books!" replied the old gentleman.

" In that case, sir," said Reginald, master-
ing with an effort a feeling of contempt
that strove to find expression on his fine
face, " in that case I must humbly submit
that we have wasted time in speaking on a
subject with which *one* of us is confessedly
unacquainted."

"Nay, young man," said the clergyman, assuming an air of dignity, "we may be acquainted with the tendency of a writer without having read all his works."

"Have you read *any one* of his books fairly and honestly through?" inquired Reginald.

"I have read extracts, and feel no inclination to read more," replied Dr. Gibson.

"Then, sir, I should very much like you to read what he says here of Martin Luther," continued Reginald.

"Not I, indeed," replied Dr. Gibson, shaking his head portentously, and waving his hand with a magisterial air; "I hope to turn my talent to better account than that. Why, the man cannot even write English! He not unfrequently concludes a member of a sentence, or even a sentence itself, with a preposition!—And as for the degrees of comparison, all the profound

grammarians who have enriched our language with the results of their wisdom and
industry might as well have never existed,
if this Mr. Carlyle is to be set up as a model
for imitation."

"I cannot dispute what you say, sir,"
said Reginald; and he was about to add
some other remark, slyly to provoke the
old gentleman, when Ellen, who had been
listening attentively, while her fingers were
employed on some bit of ornamental needle-
work, and who had been watching for an
opportunity to break off an unprofitable
discussion, suddenly uttered a little scream.

It had the desired effect. Reginald flew
to her side to see what was the matter,—it
was only a wasp that had threatened to
settle on her hand; but the wasp had to be
pursued, and ruthlessly killed; and by the
time that was accomplished, she had put the
bone of contention out of sight, and spread
the table with Latin books, and treatises

on mathematics, algebra, and geometry, enough to fully occupy any two human minds.

When the lesson was ended, and the doctor gone, Reginald, instead of plunging into a book, as was his usual habit, began to walk up and down the room.

" I wonder what is coming," thought Ellen, who knew his movements, and could read them as a pilot does the signs of the weather; " he is making up his mind about something, I can see. He will come and tell me presently what it is;—something about Dr. Gibson, I feel certain."

She was right in her conjecture. After a lengthened promenade he placed a chair resolutely before her with the back towards her, sat down crossways, with his chin resting on his hands and his elbows on the chair back and said, " Ellen !"

" Yes, Reginald," she replied, quietly, looking up from her book.

"What's to be the next move?" he inquired.

"How can I tell?" she replied—"unless it be check to the bishop?"

"Something of that sort, I believe, it must be," said he. "I have lost faith in Dr. Gibson. He is a bigot."

"I fear he is over-hasty in his judgments," replied Ellen. "I have been reading the book which he condemned so summarily, and I must confess it seems to me to breathe a religion truly catholic. The author finds that there was something true, something consequently to have faith in, even in the old Scandinavian mythology. I like that universal, tolerant spirit; it is so much more Christian than a too close adhesion to the tenets of the particular sect in which cne happens to have been brought up."

"And you are the daughter of a clergyman of the Established Church who say this!" exclaimed Reginald.

"Among my father's friends," she replied, "were a Roman Catholic priest, a Unitarian minister, a Baptist minister, and a Scottish Presbyterian preacher of the John Knox stamp; and all these used to meet beneath our roof in perfect amity."

"When I go to London," said Reginald, with a provoking twist of his mouth, "I will look out for the Happy Family, and then I shall be able to form some idea of the state of things you describe. And now to return to the question under immediate discussion :—It is quite plain to me that I have done with Dr. Gibson, for I have lost confidence in him. What shall I do next, my sweet friend?"

"I think you might now go to college with advantage," said Ellen.

"True; I might," he replied. "But first I shall go to London."

"Oh, Reginald!" she exclaimed, clasping her hands in an attitude of entreaty, "will you take me with you?"

"Take you with me!" he repeated, in amazement. "My dear girl! that is an extraordinary request."

"I only want your protection as far as the railway station," she answered, blushing deeply; "the fact is, I fear your father will not let me go unless you insist upon it, and see it done."

"No; wait till I return," said Reginald. "You will be safe here till then. And yet," he added, seeing her look uneasy, "if you would feel the happier for knowing that you can get away in case of need, I will show you a way of escape, on condition that you will not use it except in the extremest necessity. Do you promise that?"

"I do promise," she replied.

"Then come along," said Reginald, and he led her out into the garden.

This garden, it may be remembered, was sheltered from the sea-breezes by a wall of rock, partly concealed by a grove of trees.

In the centre of it was a smooth, well-kept lawn, tastefully dotted with flower-beds, now in their full glory under a July sun. A small stream, fed from a neighbouring hill, fell over a rock on the side farthest from the sea and the house, and after a winding and rapid course through lawn and shrubbery, rushed with considerable force through a narrow fissure in the cliff-wall before mentioned, and so escaped to the ocean. No one would dream of entering the fissure along with the stream, for the current, suddenly reduced to so narrow a channel, seemed strong enough to carry a stout man off his legs.

"Do you see any way of escape here?" asked her conductor, when they reached the spot where the stream widened considerably in consequence of the check given to it by the subsequent narrowing of its channel.

"No, indeed I do not," said Ellen, looking up the face of the rock, where alone she thought any outlet could be found.

"You look too high," he said. "You will have to wet your feet before you get out."

"You do not mean that I shall have to go into that dreadful hole!" cried Ellen, drawing back with a shudder.

"Indeed but I do," he replied.

"It is impossible!" she said. "I should be swept away by the water, and perhaps dashed down a precipice. It is a mere mockery to talk of escaping in this direction."

"Nevertheless," said Reginald, "if escape be ever desperately necessary, this is the only practicable way."

"Why should I not get out of the house at night?" asked Ellen.

"Because the outer gate is locked every night, and the key taken to my father," replied Reginald. "Nay, so jealous has he

become of late, that I understand he locks
it with his own hand lest the servants should
deceive him."

" The dungeons!" suggested Ellen, feeling
as if the meshes of a net were gradually
closing around her. " Could I not escape
by the way you took me on *that* night?"

Reginald shook his head.

"Shortly after that time," he said, " the
door near the library was strongly secured.
I think he had some suspicion that you
meditated giving him the slip."

Ellen looked around her with frightened
eyes. Even the smooth, inaccessible face
of the rock seemed more auspicious than
that dismal chasm. Reginald, in the meanwhile, had bared his feet, and turned his
trousers up to his knees.

" Come," said he, lifting her in his arms,
" you shall go through dry-shod this time,
and if you should ever be compelled to come
by yourself—which I do not in the least

believe will be the case, or I should see you
safe off before I left the house—you will
not find the exploit so very difficult. The
bottom is firm and level, and by holding on
to the sides, there is very little danger of
slipping. Above all, you must not be in a
hurry. Feel your footing. and get a firm
hand-grip, and you will do well.

The passage indeed seemed easy enough,
for while he spoke, he landed her high and
dry in a cavern of some extent, and toler-
ably lighted from another fissure in the
rock, which was so placed as not to be
visible from the outside.

Ellen looked round her in astonishment.
The little stream, after some murmuring at
the entrance, stole quietly along one side of
the cave, and disappeared within a recess
formed by a projection of the rock. The
floor on which she stood was level, dry. and
sandy; the air was fresh and pure, but not
chilly. But the objects that most vividly

struck her attention were those that marked the place as having served for a human habitation. There was a block of stone, squared by art, and of the height and size to serve for a table, and beside it a long bench cut out of the wall; the seat, it might have been, and the bed of an anchorite, in some distant time, when the neighbouring mansion was in reality, as it still was in name, a priory. She was brought to this conclusion by the remaining monuments of man's art,—a small altar, also chiselled from the solid rock; and above it, carved in relief on the smooth surface of the wall, just where the light from the ivy-mantled aperture fell strongest, a cross, with the Divine Image upon it. The sculpture was rude, but it was easy to perceive that a rapt soul had vividly conceived what the untutored hand had striven, not quite unsuccessfully, to represent.

. "I think," said Ellen, after a long con-

templation of this object, "that our early
reformers were over-zealous in banishing
such images as this from our churches.
And yet it was doubtless well and wisely
done; since it would be difficult to distinguish between a production of mere art,
and one that, like this, was the work of in-
spiration. Oh, Reginald! ·Does not this
solemn, this awful figure, by raising your
thoughts to the Divine original, induce you
to believe—to tremble, and to pray?"

"My poor mother used often to kneel
and pray here," he said, looking sadly down
on the step of the altar where the knees of
the anchorite had worn two hollows in the
stone, "for she was born a Spaniard—a
Spanish gipsy—and was a Catholic, if anything. For myself, dear Ellen, we must
wait, and see what I shall be. I cannot
believe by an act of the will, any more than
you can love, or I cease to love by an act of the
will. There—there—don't be frightened,"

he added, soothingly, seeing that she looked startled at the mention of the word love. "I am not such a rascal as to bring you to this lonely place to talk perforce on the forbidden subject. I brought you here to show you how to make your escape, if it should ever be absolutely necessary for you to do so. Look here! It appears quite impossible to follow the course of the stream any farther, but behind this rock, you may see, or rather feel, for it is almost dark, there are some rough and steep steps. Give me your hand. There—now you have climbed to the top of this rock, you can discover those other steps skirting along the bed of the current. Be careful of your footing, for a slip here would be fatal. Now you perceive we come to the edge of the cliff, overlooking the beach and the sea."

"It was needless to exact from me a promise to use this way of escape only in a desperate extremity," said Ellen, looking in terror on the precipice beneath. "I might as well fling myself down at once as attempt to descend by any path that we see here."

"You are like our good doctor," replied Reginald, "too hasty in jumping to a conclusion. There *is* a path, though a dangerous and difficult one. Yet you may contrive to tread it safely now, with my help, and before I go I will have a rope fixed up, so that you can steady your steps by it, should you be obliged to come here alone. The first time I descended these cliffs was in my poor mother's arms. I remember it distinctly, though I was but four years old. We went out to sea in a boat, and were taken on board a ship which conveyed us to Spain. There we lived for several years, which is one reason why I spoke so little English when you came first. We lived amongst mountains and wild places, and I learnt nothing but how to shoot, and ride, and leap, and run. My mother loved me, but she loved revenge more, and she trained me to look well enough outside, but to be at heart a mere savage brute; and in this state she meant to present me to my father, as the lawful heir to his name and estates. It was a cruel revenge for some angry words he had used to her, reflecting on her gipsy birth, which he should have thought of well before he married her, but never afterwards. If she had carried out her purpose to its fullest extent, her revenge would have been horrible, for it would have fallen most heavily on an innocent victim. You may smile, if you like, at my applying that term to myself, Miss Ellen; but observe that I am speaking of the child that I *was*, not of the man that I *am*. Well—this extremity was prevented by an accident. She had a severe illness, which caused her to fear that she might die before my claim was established, and my identity proved.

She brought me to England, and we lived among the hills, sometimes with the gipsy tribes, but mostly alone; so that I almost forgot my Spanish, without learning English, for my mother spoke very little to me, intending, I fear, that I should be a mere wild man of the woods, when I returned to my father. She would show me the house from a distance, and point out the hills and steeples and farmhouses that marked the boundaries of the estate that was to be mine; and once she brought me up to the hermitage yonder, and showed me, through the crevice, the three sons of my father by his second marriage. She told me they were my enemies, and would try to keep from me the inheritance which was mine by right. Do not look so frightened, Ellen. Neither she nor I had any share in their cruel death. While I looked at them my heart warmed towards them. I thought of the wide domain that my mother had shown

me, and I said to myself, 'There is enough
to divide amongst us, and that large house
can hold us all.' In my soul I called them
brothers, and I longed to go into the garden
and join in their play. I knew that I must
not show myself to them, and I could not
find words to express to my mother what I
felt, and how I wished to make friends with
them. You have often seen a dog trying
to make known something that he could not
utter; that was just my case, and I felt the
tears rolling down my cheeks. I loved those
fair young brothers of mine! I thought of
them, in such strange incoherent fashion as
my thinking then was; I longed passionately
to see them again, to speak to them; but I
never beheld them more. You know how
they died. Mrs. Sweetman narrated that
horrible tale very faithfully."

"Good Heavens, Reginald!" cried Ellen,
indignantly, "where were you, then, that
you could hear her?"

"Not in your room, dear," he replied,
"nor did I hear it at all. My mother heard
it. There is a secret communication between
your chamber and the one where she died,
and she went through it to look at you on
the night after you were wounded, as she
had often done before, though you had not
seen her. She said she liked to hear your
prayers. She told me that Sweetman related
to you the family history, and she felt very
grateful to you for defending her when the
old woman suggested that *she* might have
poisoned my brothers. She loved you well,
Ellen, though she had never spoken to you;
but she loved you for undoing her own evil
work, and restoring her son to somewhat of
the nature of a human being. You recollect
how she spoke of that before she died, yet
not much humanised was I when I drew
that fatal trigger!"

"You say she reported Mrs. Sweetman's
narrative to you?" said Ellen; "that must

have been after she received her wound. Why was it not attended to in time?—Her life might have been saved!"

"She did not tell me she was hurt," replied Reginald, sadly; "she said she was ill, but I did not imagine that she was wounded, still less that she was near her death.   And there she lies!" he added, pointing to the base of the precipice, on the edge of which he was standing, where Ellen might have seen, had she ventured to look over, the pile of stones which marked Mrs. Hawkshawe's grave.

END OF VOL. I.

LONDON:
SAVILL AND EDWARDS, PRINTERS, CHANDOS-STREET,
COVENT-GARDEN.